MANIAC

With a journalistic career and a nervous breakdown behind him, Alec Fraser seeks some peace in his native Argyllshire village. Instead, he encounters lust, intolerance . . . and murder.

Who killed nine-year-old Mary Allen in the shadowy alley? Was a rapist at large? Or was the perpetrator of another murder creating a smokescreen?

Only able to give a vague account of his actions at the time of the killing, Alec begins to question his sanity. His only source of support is the minister's attractive sister who, with the sober Inspector Greenlees, jolts him at last into a realisation of the truth.

MANIAC

Angus MacVicar

First Published 1969
by
John Long Limited
This edition 1998 by Chivers Press
published by arrangement with
The Author

ISBN 0 7450 8527 9

British Library Cataloguing in Publication Data available

Printed and bound in Great Britain by
Redwood Books, Trowbridge, Wiltshire

1

THE pale green Cortina nosed into the gradient. The engine began to flag. Alec Fraser changed down, toed the accelerator and saw the gangling trees at the top of the hill surging towards him.

They leant across the road, pointing skeleton arms, their trunks contorted by the prevailing wind from the west. In the pale February morning they looked dry and dead; but Alec knew that sap was already stirring inside them, swelling up like the instincts that burgeon inside a man. In a few weeks a flourish of green leaves and crab-apple blossom would hide from travellers' eyes the bare ugliness beneath.

The car reached the summit of the road. Alec changed up again. In a blur of speed the trees whisked past, above and behind him. He was conscious of relief at their passing.

Beyond the brow of the hill a lay-by had been constructed for motorists who could appreciate the beauty of a country scene. He ran the car into it and stopped. He felt excited, thankful on the brink of fulfilment, like a man, long celibate, watching a woman undress.

He fumbled for a cigarette and lit it. Calmness returned. He savoured the smoke and the distant prospect of Kilcolum, the parish in which he'd been born.

The wide strath was rimmed by a ragged shoreline,

where the sea shimmered calm and pale, reflecting the sky. Tonight, in his bedroom in the old house, he would be able to hear it; and the sound of the waves, whether quiet or heavy, would, he hoped, bring him the placid sleep he had been missing.

He smoked steadily, picking out familiar places.

He saw the square white church in the centre of the village, its stumpy spire the hub of a wheel which was the parish. Did it have the same old bell, he wondered—the bell with the crack in it, salvaged from the wreck of a Norwegian schooner a hundred and fifty years ago? He'd take odds on that it had. In this secluded part of the Scottish west coast things seldom change in a hurry.

Though, come to think of it, the irregular rows of council houses jostling the old stone buildings in the village were bright and cheerful evidence that the place wasn't completely atrophied. Their existence, of course, was a kind of memorial to his dead father, who had been that rare phenomenon, a liberal laird: a non-socialist county councillor who had rejected the idea that a farm worker, given a pleasant new home, might put coals in the bath.

Another Fraser memorial was the Village Hall, whose grey asbestos roof Alec could just make out beyond the white frontage of the Post Office and Store. He remembered the night his mother had declared it open, during one of his own University vacations: the gay dance that had followed and the girl he had spent part of the night with, kissing and fumbling in a quiet corner of one of her father's barley fields.

What had happened to Jenny? She'd be twenty-eight now—his own age—and probably married to some douce farmer. The lines of a Burns song tinkled in his head: *'I'll ne'er forget that happy, happy nicht, Amang the*

6

rigs o' barley, O.' No drink, no pep pills, no sexy talk: just the onset of affection and mutual desire and a panting happiness that in the end had left them both exhausted but still virginal.

He took a long draw at his cigarette and looked away from the village. The tension eased.

A quarter of a mile from the church, between the houses and the sea, a clump of sycamores sheltered the Manse. From Peter's letters he'd learnt there was a new minister, a young bachelor straight from divinity college, whose preaching of a 'mod' morality was liable to shock some of the older parishioners.

He smiled to himself. One of these older parishioners would almost certainly be Isaac Semple, leading elder in the kirk and head of Kilcolum's only joinery and undertaking business. Many a time he'd heard his father refer to him as 'that snivelling reactionary'. Isaac must be seventy now, or coming on for it.

But wait a second. Wasn't there something else about the Semples? What had Peter written concerning Isaac's grandson, Isaac junior? Didn't drink come into it—and communism and a University career cut short on account of a girl, a girl from Kilcolum?

Alec tried to recollect the details without success. His memory was apt to be dicey these days, no doubt a by-product of his illness. In any case, what did such details matter? Parochial scandal wasn't in his line, even though he was a newspaperman. And yet—and yet he had the feeling that this particular piece of scandal was important, if not to himself at any rate to the Fraser family.

He tried to forget the pea under the mattress and to concentrate on the lighter side of the situation. The clash beween the new minister and Isaac Semple, for instance.

7

It must have been—must still be—highly diverting, like the Bishop of Southwark tangling with John Knox. A healthy sign, thought Alec, accustomed for so long in Fleet Street to dull apathy as far as religion was concerned. It suggested, too, that the folk of Kilcolum remained individuals, able and willing to think for themselves.

On the rocky slope beyond the Manse stood the doctor's house, surrounded by a walled garden. The doctor, according to Peter, was also new and young: Captain of the Golf Club, apparently, his wife a leading light in the Drama Club. Lucky for Kilcolum. New skills, new ideas were positive poles to spark life from the negative 'squareness' of such as old Isaac.

He saw the golf course, contained in a narrow ellipse flanked on one side by the old village houses and on the other by the Breckrie burn. The greens looked tiny in the distance, a necklace of pale green jewels around the Whinny Knowe, that bushy desert, that sanctuary of poachers, guilty small boys and illicit lovers.

He remembered hiding in it once himself, along with Willie the Bomber. They had been fleeing the wrath of his father, who had surprised them taking a salmon from the burn by means of a home-made net—an illegal act, even though the fishing-rights belonged to the Frasers. Luckily, the old man was short-sighted and failed to recognise them. Crawling through the undergrowth, they had escaped from his loud imprecations and flailing stick.

Alec finished his cigarette with a quick drag and flung it out into the hedgerow. The thought of Willie Mac-Naughton, once his 'bosom crony', lightened his heart. Willie had combined the duties of green-keeper on the golf course and beadle in the kirk. His stories, particu-

8

larly about the War, from which he had emerged nicknamed 'the Bomber', because of his ability to hurl grenades immense distances, were lurid and full of drama. His skill as a poacher had been fascinating to Alec as a boy, twenty years his junior and eager for knowledge outside the normal scope of a laird's younger son.

Good old Willie. After Peter, Willie was the person he was most looking forward to meeting again.

He pressed the starter. Far away, between the village and Columba's Crag to the west, he saw among trees a semicircle of farm buildings and the white glint of Kilcolum House, where he was due for lunch in ten minutes. If he didn't get a move on he'd be late.

He nosed out of the lay-by. A number of cars passed in the opposite direction, speeding towards the town ten miles away. He recognised none of them; but it occurred to him that they were probably farmers. This was Monday, and Monday had always been market day in Stewarton.

He sent the Cortina racing downhill into the rich farmlands of Kilcolum. As he passed each house and steading he tried to remember the name of the family living there, the family, which, usually for generations, had paid rent to the Frasers. It was surprising how readily some of the names came back to him—the Ronalds, the MacLeans, the MacCallums.

And the Craigs in Ardcapple, the big farm across the burn from the golf course.

Jenny Craig. That had been her name. He began to sing: '*I'll ne'er forget that happy, happy nicht, Amang the rigs o' barley, O....*'

Peter Fraser was ten years older than his brother. This was one reason why, as boys, they had been somewhat

9

apart, with friends and interests of their own. Another reason was the knowledge, drummed into them both, that Peter would one day inherit the Kilcolum estate and that Alec, therefore, must look out for himself.

Fortunately, their temperaments were well suited to this arrangement. Peter was generally staid and solid, with a countryman's understanding of the land and its seasonal changes. Alec was more volatile, more interested in people and in what his mother used to call 'the strange cantrips of the human race'.

After a spell in a public school in Edinburgh, Peter had returned to Kilcolum. Some time later, when his father died of a coronary, he had been ready to take over as a working laird, and the Fraser image and influence in the parish had continued smoothly, in a tradition stretching back almost four hundred years.

Alec had studied at Glasgow University, taken an Arts degree and gone into journalism. For seven years he had earned his living in Fleet Street, first as a reporter, then as a foreign feature writer with the *Messenger*. His mother had died of influenza six years ago, only a few months after his father. His last fleeting visit to Kilcolum had been for her funeral.

Peter and his young wife heard the Cortina in the drive and hurried out on to the steps, accompanied by two friendly spaniels. Alec was pale and thin, Peter stoutly built and healthy; but common to both was the family legacy of black hair, Roman nose and square cleft chin. According to one story, a Spaniard rescued from an Armada galleon had left his mark on the line.

The brothers shook hands, economically guarding emotion, though Peter's greeting was heartier and less inhibited than Alec's. The dogs were absently patted and dismissed.

'Now, Alec, meet my wife,' said Peter with pride. 'Answers to the name of Meg, as you know.'

Alec also knew she was only twenty-one, seventeen years younger than his brother: a tall, long-legged girl with polished chestnut hair hanging to her shoulders. Her eyes were bright blue, with an uncertain look that threatened to shade quickly into fear. This look could be accounted for, he told himself, by the obvious fact that she was pregnant. Her mini-smock of pastel blue was ineffective camouflage.

Peter hadn't wasted much time, Alec thought with a flicker of amusement: the wedding had taken place less than six months ago, while he himself was in hospital.

He shook hands with his sister-in-law and was pleased when she leant forward impulsively and kissed him. 'We're so glad you could come. Kilcolum is just the place for you to take it easy and get better.'

'I'm sure it is. But tell me something. How on earth did a smart girl like you fall for this oafish brother of mine?'

Her hand found Peter's. The uncertainty vanished from her eyes. 'He's such a nice, comfortable father-figure! Didn't you know it's the fashion nowadays for girls to marry elderly men?'

Peter slapped her bottom. 'Come off it, wench! I bet Alec's starving. Time we had lunch.'

'Of course.' She smiled, moving away. 'Take his cases up to his room and have a sherry in the study. Eats in ten minutes.'

They climbed the broad stairway. With sensuous pleasure Alec touched the smooth oak banister down which he had slid so often.

For the first time he felt optimistic about his brother's marriage. When Peter had written to tell him of his en-

11

gagement to the daughter of Dan Sillars, headmaster of the village school, he'd been surprised and even a little anxious, not only because of the difference in ages but also because Dan Sillars had the reputation in Kilcolum of being over-fond of the drink and, especially since the death of his wife, a bit of a social rebel. But Meg was charming and obviously in love with Peter. And after all, heredity was no guide to a person's character or physical make-up. Otherwise the Frasers would have a lot more to worry about than the Sillars.

In the study, Peter raised his glass. 'Here's to a happy convalescence. Do exactly what you like, when you like. No strings to the contract.'

'Thanks. It's a great feeling to be back—and in my right mind.' Alec drank, lit a cigarette and said: 'You found a winner in Meg.'

'You can say that again! I was a bit worried at first. You know how it is. After leaving school she worked as a model in a Glasgow fashion store, and I was afraid she'd find married life here a bit stuffy. But it hasn't worked out that way. She likes the country: having been brought up in Kilcolum helps, of course. What with looking after the house, keeping an eye on her father and being in the Drama Club—well, she's always up to something. I'm lucky, Alec. And luckier still that she—that she . . .'

'I know. Quick work!'

Peter grinned. 'Not due until the end of May. Well outside the illegal limit!'

'I hope it's a son and heir.'

'So does Meg. I don't give a damn myself, so long as she's all right. But look, Alec, what about you? How d'you feel?'

'Pretty good. It was foul torture while it lasted.'

12

'I thought you were a goner, that first time I went down to see you in London. Why were the doctors so cagey? What exactly was the trouble?'

'Some kind of nervous breakdown. So they tell me.'

'Any specific cause?'

Alec hesitated. He wasn't proud of the circumstances that had triggered off his illness. Nevertheless, he owed it to Peter, shrewd and understanding and his nearest kin, to confess the truth—or at least a relevant part of the truth. But was this the time for confession, at the start of a gay family reunion? He thought not.

He shrugged and said: 'Too much gadding around after stories for the *Messenger*, I expect.'

Peter gave him a straight look. 'You ought to have taken a holiday. I kept telling you.'

'Sure. But never mind, I'm perfectly well now. The specialist says six weeks in the country should make me fit for anything.'

'What about afterwards? All this commuting to Paris, Rome, Beirut . . .'

'They've appointed a new man in my place. I'm going back as a leader writer—chained to a desk, worse luck! But actually the editor has been very kind, keeping me on at all.'

'Surprising how many decent chaps there are in this hard world . . .'

'Darling, you sound like the Archbishop of Canterbury!' said Meg from the doorway. 'If you've finished your sherry I'll bring in the soup.' She eyed the decanter. 'You lucky people! How would either of you like to be pregnant, forced to give up cigarettes and drink and all other pleasurable habits?'

Peter put his arm about her. 'A nagger, that's what

she is! Come away, Alec. Let's have lunch and start the big bucolic build-up!'

That afternoon Peter had to make a quick run to Stewarton. There was an auction mart, he said, at which he planned to buy a couple of spring calving cows for the Home Farm. As he prepared to climb into the mud-stained Land Rover, he suggested that while he was away Alec might like to lie down and have a post-luncheon snooze. 'After that long drive from Glasgow this morn-ing you're bound to feel tired,' he said.

Alec laughed. 'Now look, I'm not a complete wreck! I'll help Meg wash the dishes and then walk down to the village.'

'Sure you feel up to it?'

'Oh, come on! You're an old fuss-pot!'

'Well, it's not a bad afternoon, but there's rain in the offing, so take a coat. Never mind the dishes. Meg has an old dame who helps in the kitchen. You remem-ber her—Mrs MacKay, the shoemaker's widow?'

'I remember.'

'I think I told you in a letter about Nancy, her daugh-ter? Nancy MacKay—she'd only be a schoolgirl when you went to the University. Afterwards she worked here as a maid, first with Mother and then with my house-keeper. Well, not long after Mother died, Nancy found herself in the family way and the blame fell on young Isaac Semple. There was a hell of a row, caused mostly by old Isaac, as you can imagine. One day they found her in the burn, under the Ardcapple bridge: you know, between the farm and the village. One of the wooden handrails on the bridge was broken, and at the Inquiry the jury returned a verdict of accidental death, though some queer rumours were floating around. It just about

14

finished Mrs MacKay at the time, but she's got over it now, and I try to make up for things by paying her good wages. Luckily Meg and she are great buddies.'

Alec nodded. There was a knot in his stomach, and he couldn't trust himself to speak. His memory was no longer at fault. He scarcely noticed the curious harshness in his brother's voice and the shimmer of pain in his eyes.

'I just wanted to remind you,' Peter said, 'so that if you get talking with Mrs MacKay you won't say anything that might—well, that might bring back unhappy memories.'

He got into the Land Rover and started the engine. 'Enjoy your walk,' he said, more naturally. 'If you run into your old pal Willie the Bomber don't let him lead you astray!'

He let in the clutch, smiling, and the Land Rover crunched off on to the farm road.

Alec stared after it, trying to control the tension in his body. A flock of starlings crackled past with a swish of displaced air. They wheeled up on busy wings, turned and settled on the roof of the house. He listened to their chatter.

Then he became aware of a noisy tractor in the field behind the house, where one of Peter's three hired men was ploughing. Prosaic reality smoored the flames of recollection.

Feeling better, he went inside, had a word with Meg and collected his waterproof.

2

As he approached the village, climbing up from the burnside track, he saw to his left, mowing on the ninth green, a burly man approaching fifty, bald-headed, with a congested red face and an even redder walrus moustache.

'Willie!' he yelled, climbing the fence.

The big man paused and looked up. For a second or two he remained motionless, obviously puzzled. Then his lugubrious face was transformed by a smile. He switched off the mower motor, raised his hand in delight and galloped across the green.

'Alec Fraser!' he bellowed, hoarsely.

'Willie, you old scoundrel!'

They shook hands.

'Alec, am I glad to see you! From all reports you were either dead or dying! But I knew fine my old buddy wouldna die that easy. Down for a holiday?'

'More or less. Doctor's orders.'

'Why the hell did you come in February? I'm sure you know the salmon dinna start running in the Breckrie till the month o' May!'

'I couldn't pick my time, Willie.' Alec produced a packet of cigarettes. As they lit up he said: 'But maybe we can manage a round or two of golf?'

'Any day o' the week, son. As long as the course is kept tidy to the satisfaction o' the Committee, my time's my own.'

'Big shot, eh?'

'Well, I've come up in the world since you saw me last. William MacNaughton, Greenkeeper and Professional: it's painted up on the shop next to the clubhouse. My mother and I live in the wee cottage yonder, at the clubhouse gate.'

'Good for you, Willie! The club has surely come up in the world, too?'

'Oh, ay. We get a big crowd o' summer visitors nowadays. And there's a one-armed bandit in the bar. Our income is near five times what it used to be.'

'You know, that surprises me in Kilcolum.'

'New brooms, Alec. Dr Young has modern ideas, and now that he's Captain the old squares are taking a back seat. Then there's Commander Heathergill. He's a hellish efficient Secretary.'

Alec said: 'Commander Heathergill?'

'Retired naval bloke,' explained Willie. 'His wife has a lang pedigree and plenty o' money. About five years ago he built the new bungalow up there, beside the doctor's house. Damns and blasts like a navvy, but if you play fair wi' him, he plays fair wi' you. Reminds me a wee bit o' your father, Alec.'

'High-powered stuff! But in spite of it all I take it you're still the beadle?'

'Och, sure. Me and Mr Thomson—that's the new minister—we're just like that.' He held up two calloused fingers, awkwardly crossed.

'You mean he hasn't rumbled you yet?'

Willie gave a small, deprecating laugh. 'Och, there's nothing to rumble nowadays. I'm getting so old and stiff.'

'Come off it!'

'Well, anyway, I never did like going it alone, and since you went away there's been naebody else with a yen for the poaching. The young lads hereabouts are no' what they were. A lot o' damned cissies. Bowls or

17

badminton, that's the height o' their ambition. No' like you were, Alec, daft for adventure. D'you mind the ploys we had, on dark nights down by the burn?'

'I do indeed! You with the gaff, me with the net.'

'Two bob a pound he used to give us—John MacNair the fishmonger in Stewarton. Old skinflint!'

'I don't know about you, Willie, but I was glad to get it. Kept me in pocket-money at the University.'

'Och, in them days I liked a wee bit extra cash myself!'

'We certainly earned it. Some near shaves we had!'

'You're telling me! D'you mind the time we were spotted by old Isaac Semple, down near the Ardcapple bridge? How long ago was that? About ten years maybe. Why did he no' report us, Alec? He recognised us all right. It's a thing that puzzles me to this day.'

'Well, I think he had somebody with him.'

'So you've aye said.'

'I'm sure of it, Willie. I saw a movement in the dark, in the bushes beyond the bridge.'

'Maybe it was a lassie! Maybe the old hypocrite was scared to tell on us in case we'd tell on him!'

They laughed together. Neither of them gave a moment's credence to this picture of Kilcolum's leading elder being caught out in a clandestine affair. To their irreverent minds it was simply a happy and intriguing thought, like the idea of General de Gaulle slipping on a banana skin.

Willie said: 'There's no' much real excitement in Kilcolum nowadays. If you forget about the sheep.'

Alec looked up, sharply. 'What sheep?'

'Och, you'll no' have heard. It happened just the other day. One o' Archie Craig's ewes. In lamb she was. He found her in the field yonder, on the other side o' the

18

bridge, dead as a door-nail. The vet said she'd been strangled.'

To Alec the afternoon was suddenly cold and raw. Pleasant memories began to disappear under a slow tide of ugly nausea. He looked up. He saw the track down from the village, the white-painted bridge, the track leading across the field, past the cottage and up to the farm. The field was under grass. He remembered it best as a sea of ripe barley, rippling in the moonlight.

He shivered and said: 'But surely that's impossible, Willie? It's incredible, inhuman.'

'Ay, it caused a bit o' a sensation. But if you ask me, the vet's no' a hundred per cent reliable. Maybe he had a dram in him. Who the hell would want to strangle a sheep?'

Behind them erupted a shout of 'Fore!' Startled, they looked back along the ninth fairway, where a plump young man in a white sweater and black flannels, accompanied by a girl, was waiting to play his approach shot.

'Speak o' the de'il!' said Willie, as they moved quickly to the rough behind the green. 'It's the minister on his day off. Minister's Monday he calls it. A demon for the golf is Mr Thomson, but he'll never get his handicap down till he learns to swing at the ball and no' to bash it. Look at yon!'

Turf scattered as the minister used an 8-iron like a baseball bat. The ball floated up in a weak parabola and landed well short of the green.

'Who's the girl?' said Alec, deliberately closing his mind to everything except the present.

'His sister. She keeps house for him.' Willie's eyes were warm, like an affectionate spaniel's. 'Kate Thomson, a peach o' a lassie. Watch this.'

She looked lithe and slim in her grey polo-necked

19

sweater and dark blue golfing slacks; but as she swung lazily into the ball Alec was conscious of a basic sturdiness and strength. He was even more conscious, however, of her thick and beautiful dark red hair.

The ball fell on the soft green, jumped a foot forward and spun back, only a yard from the pin.

He said: 'I've paid good money to see professionals do worse.'

'She played for Glasgow University, so they tell me.' Willie was hoarsely secretive now, as the couple came close. 'She was teaching in Glasgow till Mr Thomson got the parish, then she gave it up to look after him. They made her President o' the Kilcolum Youth Club. No wonder it's flourishing!' He leered behind his hand. 'The young fellows come flocking round her like randy bees after a queen.'

The Rev. Harry Thomson essayed a chip. This time he soled the ball and it skimmed left on a low trajectory. It struck the mower lying deserted on the green, glanced back to the right but still lay farther from the hole than his sister's.

'No' in your usual form today, sir,' said Willie, with more than a hint of sycophancy. He ambled forward, followed by Alec, and took out the flag-stick. 'Miss Kate had a beauty, though!'

She took her putter from her bag, laughing. 'He's going to be five down in a minute, and he doesn't like it!'

The minister looked more like a well-fed young business man than an aesthetic clergyman. He tugged at his tweed cap. 'You put me off, Willie. I'm not used to a gallery.'

To prove it, he missed his putt. Kate sank hers.

'Never mind, sir,' Willie sympathised. 'You sank some

20

good ones in the kirk yesterday. Yon was a grand sermon!'

The Rev. Harry grinned at Alec. 'Part of his duty as beadle. Keeping up the minister's morale.'

'Och, but wait!' Willie remembered his social duty. 'Miss Kate, this is Mr Alec Fraser, the laird's brother. Come for a wee holiday. He's no' been so well.'

'I guessed it. There's a strong family resemblance.'

Since news travels far and fast, even from London to a quiet backwater in Argyll, she had listened to plenty of gossip about the nature of his illness and its cause. There was curiosity, therefore, in her dark green eyes but none of the incipient fear that had lurked in Meg's.

The minister rushed in, a man of God yet also of the people, determinedly offering an assurance that no matter what had occurred in the past, he at any rate, as a 'mod' Christian, was prepared to be tolerant and friendly with anybody. 'I'm terribly glad to meet you, Mr Fraser. I've always enjoyed your articles in the *Messenger*. Your foreigners are real people, not the figures of quaint fun or of unredeemed vice we so often hear about from correspondents in the reactionary papers. You must gen me up about the present situation in Egypt. Kate and I were born there. My father had an accountancy business in Alexandria until Nasser threw us out.'

Kate said: 'I hope the Kilcolum air does you good, Mr Fraser.' His paleness worried her. 'You'll get well fed, that's for sure. Meg is a wizard cook.'

There was something about her, something cool and sensible and kind, that stirred his heart. She would never blame him, he felt sure, without listening first to his side of the story. She might even understand it and offer him comfort.

But he disciplined the emotion and said: 'I sampled

21

Meg's cooking at lunch. Superb. As for the good air of Kilcolum, it's made a difference already.'

Banality, that was it. Avoid excitement and involvement. Let the brain lie fallow. The doctors were wise, and he'd follow their advice.

Round the bushes on the Whinny Knowe another two golfers appeared on the ninth fairway.

The Rev. Harry said: 'Well, we musn't hold up the course. Remember, Mr Fraser, we keep open house at the Manse. Do come and spend an evening with us, if you have time.'

'Meg and I will make the arrangements.' Kate smiled at Alec, and he felt a pleasurable lifting of responsibility. Then—'Come on, Harry,' she said, moving towards the tenth tee. 'Face up to the slaughter like a man!'

When they had driven off, Willie said: 'What did I tell you! A wee smasher, eh?'

Alec nodded, still wary of involvement. 'Not bad.'

'No' bad?' Willie was shocked. 'Ten years ago Alec Fraser had a hungrier eye for a lassie than that!'

'Dead days, Willie. Dead days gone beyond recall.'

'Quoting poetry next! You're in a bad way, son. We'll need to do something about it. First tee tomorrow afternoon—two o'clock, eh?'

'Fine.'

'We'll have you roarin' about like a young stag in no time. Wait till you see!'

He went up to the village by way of Riverside Street and Fisher Row. It was now after five o'clock, and behind thin grey clouds the sun was edging down over Columba's Crag. A spit of rain was beginning to fall. He put on his waterproof.

Tea-time smoke plumed up from the chimneys. Some

22

of the farm-workers were coming home, the elderly ones on push-bikes, a few of the younger men roaring in on motor-scooters.

Children not long released from school were scattered on the roadway, the girls playing hopscotch on one leg, the boys racing about after an old football. Alec had the sensation of being a ghost. He moved on with the shouting in his ears and the ball bouncing against his legs, but he felt remote from this world of engrossing play. He was willing to speak and be friendly, but they were uninterested. He was a stranger and therefore condemned to be ignored.

He turned into the Main Street, near the church, and went towards the Hall and the white-fronted Store. He met housewives with shopping-baskets, some of them with prams as well. The majority didn't even glance his way. Two of the more elderly ladies recognised him and smiled, shyly, and he stopped and talked and was absurdly grateful for their recognition. But they seemed unwilling to spend more than a few seconds with him. They were uneasy, nervous. Maybe they were anxious to get home to make their husbands' tea.

He tried to rationalise his disappointment. He had come back expecting to find Kilcolum as it had been when he was a boy. He must now recognise, however, that conditions, even in the country, are never static. People change. They grow older and forget. In an affluent society the old virtues of neighbourliness and hospitality tend to be overlooked. Put romance and nostalgia aside, he told himself, and, as a therapeutic exercise, consider the parish of today with cool journalistic objectivity.

Thirty or forty years ago the Kilcolum farmers had been hard-wrought and poor, little more than peasants. Now, thanks to grants and subsidies, most of Peter's

23

tenants were comparatively wealthy, with a standard of living at least as comfortable as the laird's. Owning high-grade cars and batteries of modern agricultural implements, they enjoyed as much leisure as any business man and followed a much healthier way of life.

Their women-folk, too, well educated and well nourished, had the support of every kind of labour-saving gadget. No longer were they slatternly slaves, worn out before they were fifty by milking, cheese-making and child-bearing.

As for the farm-workers, in the old days they had huddled at night in damp, broken-down stone cottages, existing precariously at subsistence level. In this era of higher wages, better medical and educational facilities, modern rent-subsidised council houses and well-balanced school meals, they were much better off in fact than their employers had been in the bad old days of agricultural slump. Alec himself, though not yet thirty, remembered ragged children at school, pale and thin from malnutrition. The children in Kilcolum today were rosy-cheeked and sturdy, as well if not better clad than children in the cities.

Here was a social theme, he struggled to convince himself, ripe for popular treatment in the *Messenger* leader page.

But his mind was inefficiently geared to the effort of sustaining such an impersonal line of thought. Gradually his objectivity declined. The problem of Kilcolum's reaction to his presence became subjective again.

He had looked forward to coming home, to mixing with the folk of the village and drawing courage and strength from their old-fashioned friendship. But to the majority he was a stranger, and it appeared that to the few who did remember him he was a creature who

24

merited only suspicious concern. He began to wonder how many details of his misfortune had percolated through from London.

He was grateful, of course, that Peter and Willie were prepared to take him back at a former valuation. But there was an ambiguity about his reception by almost everybody else that daunted him. He was aware of tension in his muscles and the onset of a headache; and though the day was moderately cold his hands became clammy with sweat.

A young woman on high heels, carrying a string grocery bag and wearing a short red skirt and green quilted anorak, passed him on her way towards the Ardcapple bridge. Her careless brown hair was protected by a scarlet headscarf.

He stopped. 'Jenny!' he exclaimed.

Her back stiffened. She halted, as if reluctantly, and turned. Flushing vividly, she said: 'Hullo, Alec.'

She wore discreet make-up. Her figure was slim, lacking the plumpness he remembered. She still looked young and desirable, but the innocent eagerness of ten years ago was no longer there. Her eyes held wordly knowledge and even a hint of defiance. It didn't occur to him to find in her almost painful blush evidence of a lingering vulnerability.

His mouth was suddenly dry and salty with the echo of desire. His voice shook as he said: 'How are you, Jenny?'

The blush faded, leaving her cheeks paler than before. 'I'm fine. But you, Alec—I heard you were ill. Are you better?'

'Yes. I'm here for six weeks' convalescence.'

He remembered her kisses, prim, pursed kisses merging into parted lips clinging to his own. He remembered her response to his hand on her bare breasts, trembling at first then eager and in the end almost fiercely insistent. He remembered the moaning in her throat at the increasing intimacy of his caresses. He remembered her hands on him, the voilence of his desire and the violence of his disappointment at its sudden involuntary realease while he still struggled ineffectually with her clothes.

But he remembered also the affection and concern that had subdued the violence. They had loved each other again and soon she, too, had experienced release. And afterwards they had lain quietly in the barley, holding each other until the moon went down and the chill air of dawn told them it was time to go home.

Did Jenny remember? He had no means of telling. There appeared to be a barrier between them now, invisible, undefinable. They were complete strangers, he thought, with nothing in common but one night of sexual adventure. In their stilted conversation he discovered an undertone of tragedy.

'You must pay us a visit at Ardcapple. My father and mother would like to see you.'

'You still live at home?'

'Most of the time. I'm a teacher, in the school here.'

They looked at each other. He decided that his desire was only a memory of desire. She was a woman of experience now, wary and suspicious. He could see no interest in her eyes, no interest at any rate in his masculinity. He looked down at the hand which held the string bag and saw a glint of diamonds on her engagement finger. The tension in his stomach became a small sickness. Like everybody else Jenny was remote, unwilling to relax in the glow of a former relationship.

And yet the blush was returning. 'Alec,' she said,

anxiously, 'are you really better? You seem—different somehow.'

'So do you, Jenny.'

'Do I?' She put her free hand on his arm. He shied away from it. She said: 'Come and see us, anyway. Any night except a Thursday. I teach an evening class on a Thursday.'

'Thank you.'

'Au revoir, then. Be good to yourself.'

'Au revoir.'

She turned away, almost as reluctantly as she had turned towards him. He watched her as she went along the street, moving with firm short steps towards the alley and the bridge below. In his head was a muzzy pain; in his heart an emptiness.

Lacrimae rerum. Tears for the might-have-been.

3

THE muzziness wore away. The pain became localised. It was an old enemy. The doctors had told him it would probably recur for some time yet, especially if he allowed himself to become over-excited. Nothing to worry about, they had assured him: simply a warning that nerves exposed to a long period of strain were still raw and should be cosseted. In the peaceful, undemanding atmosphere of the country, according to their diagnosis, it would generally wear off within an hour or so.

He saw a sign hanging outside a plain-faced building. Fresh paint outlined two crossed keys and a galleon.

27

Beneath the galleon was the legend, THE FRASER ARMS. A dram might hasten the cure, he decided. He looked at his wristwatch. It was after half-past five. The cocktail bar would now be open.

The first person he saw in the cosy glow was Dan Sillars, Meg's father. Lean and loose-boned, he was sitting on a high stool, with a pint tankard of draught beer at one elbow. Hollow, carelessly shaven cheeks and a baldness untidily camouflaged by straggling iron-grey hair made him appear older than his fifty years. The lapels of his dark blue suit were sprinkled with cigarette-ash; his trouser-legs were baggy. He hadn't changed much, Alec thought, though maybe the deep-set blue eyes—eyes inherited by Meg—were now a little more dull and bloodshot than they once had been.

To the fair-haired man beside him he was saying, loudly: 'It's virtually an open sewer, man! Seepage from Ronald's midden runs straight into it.'

'But it's *outside* your playground wall.'

'Germs can fly over walls.'

'Not the kind of germs that cause epidemics . . .'

'Look! If germs can't fly, kids can climb! They could easily fall into that drain and pick up God knows what hellish diseases! All I'm asking is that you should recommend piping. The Council will listen to you, as the local doctor . . .'

In mid-speech he caught a glimpse of Alec moving in towards the counter. He looked up and blinked. Then, with a quick, awkward movement, he came off the stool.

'Young Fraser! Man, glad to see you!' He slapped his shoulder. 'Meg told me you were coming. How's the health?'

'Fairish.'

'Have a drink?'

28

'Thanks. A small whisky.'

'Sure. Hey, Isaac,' he gestured to the white-coated barman, 'a Scotch and soda for Mr Fraser.' He put a bony hand on Alec's arm, peered at him and said: 'You look peakish, son, peakish. But here's the man to put you right if you need him. Dr Jimmy Young. A buddy of mine, even though he's a stubborn cuss. Jimmy, this is Alec Fraser, Peter's young brother.'

At a guess, the new doctor was about his own age. About his own height, too, though stouter and more strongly built, with an easy smile. It occurred to Alec that the smooth ruddiness of his cheeks was somehow out of place in a bar. Anyway, what was a doctor doing in the Fraser Arms at this time of day?

'I dragged him in to discuss a public scandal,' said Dan, as if divining the question. 'The open drain running past the school. Look, Alec, you've had some recent experience of doctors. Wouldn't you say that on the whole they're a lot of damned reactionaries?'

Dr Young laughed. Dutifully Alec laughed, too. The arrival of his drink enabled him to avoid answering.

The doctor said: 'Wouldn't you say, Mr Fraser, that on the whole teachers are a lot of damned revolutionaries?'

'*Slainte!*' Alec raised his glass. 'I refuse to hold the jackets!'

'Wise man!' said Jimmy Young. Taking a sip from his half pint of export, he kept watching Alec's face as if interested in what he saw there.

The whisky soothed the pain. When had he arrived in Kilcolum? What were his plans? Automatically he answered the conventional questions. Something else had begun to worry him. That barman, that reedy young man with the dark eyes and long black side-pieces: surely he ought to know him? There was something reminiscent about his gaunt seriousness, about the raw, big-boned hands lifting and polishing a row of glasses.

Isaac? Of course. This was old Isaac Semple's grandson. This was the boy who'd been blamed for Nancy MacKay's 'misfortune', who'd been blasted from his perch at Glasgow University by the righteous wrath of his grandfather: wrath directed not only at his liaison with a servant girl but also at his 'communistic' ideas and addiction to the bottle. This was Isaac junior. How on earth had he become a barman in the Fraser Arms? Surely it was a situation which must offend his 'unco guid' grandfather?

But such questions were momentarily forgotten as a picture came into his mind. Brought into being by Peter's story and highlighted by his recognition of Isaac junior, it was a picture of the high Ardcapple bridge, white wood showing in a splintered rail and a girl in the river below, her body snagged against a rock, her mousy hair streaming like weed in the water.

He gulped down what remained of his whisky. The pain in his head didn't seem to be getting any worse. In fact, it might even be passing. It was folly to dwell on old scandals, on the dire consequences of the sins of the flesh. Better have another dram and establish the cure.

He said: 'You'll have a whisky with that cold beer, Dan. Warm it up a bit. You, too, Dr Young?'

The doctor waved a muscular, well-manicured hand. 'No, thank you. I'm due home at six. My wife is expecting me ...'

'Oh, come on, Jimmy!' said Dan, interrupting brashly. 'Alice won't mind if you're a wee bit late. Anyway, you don't have a surgery on a Monday evening, and it's not often we get a chance to celebrate the return of a native.'

'Well, just a small one, Mr Fraser.'

'Sure.' Alec turned to the barman. 'Three whiskies, please.' As the drink was being poured, he said: 'You're Isaac Semple, I think?'

'That's right, Mr Fraser.' A tentative smile softened the hard facial contours.

'How's your grandfather?'

'Fit as usual. I don't see much of him nowadays, except in the street.'

'So you're not in the business?'

He shook his head. 'I got married some years ago, and Virginia and I live our own lives. This barman job helps us rub along.' He finished dispensing and gave Alec his change. Lowering his voice, he said: 'I hope sometime I can have a chat with you, Mr Fraser. You see, I—I'm having a go as a freelance journalist, and a word of advice from you would be a tremendous help.'

That Isaac junior should show such independence and such cool disregard for the dictates of his grandfather was astonishing. That he should have stuck it out in Kilcolum after the Nancy MacKay affair—and found a girl willing to marry him—was even more astonishing. But that old Isaac's grandson, last of a long line of 're-spectable' tradesmen, should go in for writing was to Alec the most astonishing thing of all.

He studied Isaac's face. It was broad and bony, with the dour look characteristic of his clan. And yet the eyes were clear and intelligent, offering a friendliness that had never been apparent in old Isaac's.

Two commercial travellers entered the bar and rapped the counter for attention.

'We'll have a chat,' Alec promised. 'It requires courage to start up as a freelance these days. But you've got plenty of that, I imagine.'

Unwilling to risk becoming involved with the commercial travellers, Dan and the doctor had left the counter and taken seats at a small table in a corner. Alec carried the drinks across. They toasted him.

Dan said: 'So you remembered young Isaac?'

'I spotted the family likeness.'

'He told you he wants to become a writer?'

'Yes. What's the story? Sounds off-beat to me.'

Swallowing a mouthful of beer, the schoolmaster said: 'You've got to face it, Alec—Kilcolum today isn't the douce, cosy place you probably think you remember. The young folk here are like the young folk everywhere else: rebellious, unconventional, unsure of themselves in one way, confident in another. They buck against intolerance, against the materialism of modern politics, against war and the atom bomb. They go searching for moral standards, which in these days are damned hard to find.'

Drink was making him loquacious. He gulped down his whisky and went on: 'It's against this background you must consider young Isaac's story, not the background of feudal submission which existed in Kilcolum for so long. Today you face things, Alec, bring them stark into the open and, if possible, exorcise them.'

'And—and that's what Isaac did?'

Dan nodded. 'He denied absolutely that he had ever slept with Nancy MacKay. She was an attractive kid in a pert, untutored kind of way, and he sometimes partnered her at dances and saw her home to Kilcolum House, where, as you remember, she was working at the time. But he steadfastly refused to admit any responsibility for her condition.'

32

Alec's hands were becoming clammy again. The pain in his head was knifing back. He said: 'His grandfather didn't believe him?'

'Of course not. Old Isaac thinks in black and white and always prefers black if there's a choice. He ranted and raved like John Knox at a Holy Fair. He kept saying how glad he was that young Isaac's parents were dead. Had they been alive they'd never have recovered from the disgrace. Then he issued his verdict. He'd cut off his grandson's University allowance, bring him back to Kilcolum and make him shrive his sins by working as an apprentice in the joinery and undertaking business. He told the Kirk Session that his grandson's fornication was a result of loose living among drunken communists in the city and that he'd see to it that the boy was never exposed to such influences again.'

'No prodigal son stuff about old Isaac,' said Jimmy Young, who seemed to have forgotten about his wife.

'Right. But the remarkable thing is that though young Isaac did come home, soon after Nancy was drowned, he only stayed a few months under his grandfather's control. One day they had a row about wages. Part of it was overheard by half a dozen workers in the joinery shop and on the whole it seems to have been a fantastic bust-up. Old Isaac took to his bed for a week, ostensibly with 'flu, while young Isaac went off and brought back a bride, a girl he'd met in Glasgow while at the University.'

Dan coughed, lubricated his throat with beer and continued: 'You know the old cottage on Ardcapple Farm, Alec, on the other side of the bridge? Well, Archie Craig let them have it, decent man that he is. They restored and furnished it together, and there they are still, living on young Isaac's earnings as a barman and freelance journalist. Seems his wife had secretarial training and now does typing on the side. But what she makes can't amount to much.'

The doctor rose and said: 'My turn, gentlemen! Whiskies, I take it?' His face was flushed. It looked heavier, less professionally contained.

Dan said: 'Sure, Jimmy!'

Alec's head was throbbing, and he was finding it difficult to concentrate on the story. 'Yes, please,' he said, absently.

When the doctor moved away, carrying the empty glasses, he wrinkled his forehead at the schoolmaster. 'How d'you explain it?' he said. 'This—this transformation, I mean.'

'Sounds odd, uncharacteristic of Kilcolum! I grant you that. But as I said, times are changing, and the fact is that by now young Isaac has succeeded in living down his past—if ever he had a past. He drinks very little, and though his opinions are decidedly left-wing, he doesn't ram them down people's throats. He's popular in the parish, and so is his wife Virginia, who is straightforward and sociable and helps out with the neighbours' children. Seems a pity she hasn't yet had a baby of her own.'

Suddenly Dan looked stern, pointed a magisterial finger and said: 'I'll tell you this much. The majority of people in Kilcolum are now quite satisfied that young Isaac was telling the truth about Nancy MacKay. She was in the family way all right, but it wasn't his fault.'

'But—but old Isaac . . .'

'Now we come to the strangest part of the story.' Dan frowned and drank more beer. 'From the time they had their row to the present day,' he said, 'grandfather and grandson have scarcely ever spoken to each other. Frankly I don't understand it. You'd think old John

34

Knox would have been inclined to persecute the boy who dared to stand up to him. But no. Strange as it may seem, Alec, I believe he's scared of young Isaac.'

'Scared?'

'Yes. Mind you, old windbags are sometimes liable to quick deflation when challenged by a clear conscience and honesty of purpose. Anyway, young Isaac's case is interesting, psychologically. Had he gone into his shell and allowed inhibitions to build up inside him like water behind a dam, God knows what might have happened. The Semples have always been prone to violence. Old Isaac's uncle was jailed for manslaughter—striking an employee with an adze. But young Isaac refused to take refuge either in guilty silence or in cutting himself off from his neighbours. He acted openly and honestly, and people have now come to accept him at his own valuation.'

He paused, a crooked smile taking years off his age. He shrugged and said: 'If all this sounds like a sermon, Alec, forgive me. I may be wrong, all along the line, but I don't think so. At school young Isaac was dour and contained, like all the Semples, but behind it I could detect cleverness and a wish to be affable. He wrote a first-class essay, and I am not surprised he's taken up journalism.'

The doctor came back with the whiskies. They drank to him.

He began to talk about golf, pointing out that in his opinion the best way to exorcise inhibitions was to take part in a keen four-ball. Inevitably, Dan had a sarcastic response. 'Golf!' he snorted. 'Grown men trying to put a wee ball into a wee hole and swearing when they can't! Give me strength!'

As Captain of the Kilcolum Club, Jimmy Young

plunged into the argument, which both he and Dan obviously enjoyed.

Alec offered a word here and there, but his mind drifted from the subject. He was thinking that in several ways young Isaac's case resembled his own. But, according to Dan, young Isaac had let all his guilt and bitter regret come to the surface, deliberately bursting the dam of his emotional resistance. This was what he himself hadn't done, and inside him a flood was rising against the dam, so powerfully that his head now seemed incapable of containing it.

A stiffness affected his body, like a fever. Far from alleviating his condition, another three rounds of whisky appeared to make it worse. Words and laughter, heat and cigarette-smoke billowed round him like the background of a dream. In the tale of *Tam O'Shanter* 'the night drave on wi' sangs an' clatter, an' aye the ale was growing better'. In his case the reverse was true. He became sick of the taste of whisky. The pain in his head developed into a violent ache. The conviction grew on him that something was about to happen, some ghastly event that would remind him of the night Elizabeth had died.

It was nearly eight o'clock when they decided to leave the hotel. They stood on the pavement under the swinging sign, hitching up the collars of their coats.

Thin, slanting rain out of a pitch-black sky glinted in the light of the street lamps. The cold and wet and the freshness of the country air caused his headache to burgeon into a moment of wild dizziness. He stumbled towards the kerb and would have fallen had it not been for Dr Young's supporting arm.

Dan said: 'Look, Alec, my flat is only a block away. I'll get out the car and ...'

'I'm all right.' The shock of his near-collapse had steadied him. 'I walked here. I'll walk back. I know the way.'

'But Peter and Meg would expect me to look after you. It's not as if you were fully fit ...'

'To hell with Peter and Meg!' He was experiencing an unexpected diminution of the pain. Euphoria possessed him. He laughed. 'And I keep telling you, I'm not an invalid. Good grief, it's less than a mile to Kilcolum House if I take the short-cut by Ardcapple.' He thrust a hand against the doctor's shoulder. 'Tell him, Jimmy—tell Danny Boy I don't require a nursemaid.'

Their heads were swimming. Laphroaig on empty stomachs is potent medicine.

Jimmy Young said: 'No need to bring Dan into it. My car's in Fisher Row. I'd be glad to give you a lift— not as a doctor, as a friend.'

'Come off it! Your house is in the opposite direction. Anyway, your wife is expecting you.' Alec giggled. 'She's been expecting you for a long time now!'

'Listen to me, son!' Dan put on his headmaster act. 'We're all a bit tiddley. We're in an argumentative mood. At the same time, it's dark and it's raining, and there's a wind getting up ...'

'Listen yourself, Danny Boy! I'm extremely obliged to you both. But I—I'm not worried about the dark or about a spot of rain and wind. Bucolic, that's me. Hundreds of times I've used that track. Once there was a barley field on the other side of the bridge. I knew it well. Too well, maybe!'

Passing pedestrians noticed them huddled together, talking with raised voices. They offered curious glances and then, for the time being, forgot about it. Raised voices were not uncommon outside the Fraser Arms.

Suddenly Alec broke away and began to walk with vigour in the direction of the bridge. For a moment, at a loss, the other two looked after him. Then, with a shrug of resignation, the doctor said: 'Let him be, Dan. He's a bit on edge, still suffering from the effects of his illness. Frustration at this point could be bad for him.'

'Something in that.'

'Physically he's fit enough. Well, good night, Dan. For all the distance I think I'll walk home, too. No good risking a breathalyser test from Constable Reid. I'll collect my car in the morning.'

'Sure. Good night, Jimmy. Remember what I said about Ronald's drain.'

In the abrupt way of men under the influence, they parted, Dan striding off towards his flat in the high tenements behind the Hall, the doctor in the opposite direction, towards his modern bungalow on the outskirts of the village.

4

THE cold wind fanned his face. Rain washed away the sweaty stuffiness of the cocktail bar.

His headache had temporarily lifted and he was feeling good. This was the way with migraine, the specialist had told him. A coming and a going of pain, its intensity varied and incalculable. He must suffer it for some time yet, but before long the ragged nerve-ends would heal and his condition would return to normal. A short while ago he had been cursing himself for drinking too much; but maybe his session with Dan and the doctor hadn't been such bad medicine after all. Under its influence, aided now by the cleansing keenness of the air of Kilcolum, his confidence was coming to the surface.

He made straight for the dark alley leading down to the bridge. He was aware of figures hastening past on the street but only with the outer fringes of his mind.

As he drew abreast of the Hall lights blazed at the entrance and a number of little girls came running out, dressed in Brownie uniforms. They separated, laughing and calling to one another. Some raced on ahead of him, their shoes splashing on the wet pavement. Some climbed into two cars which had been waiting by the kerb.

He passed the church, its white walls floodlit by a cluster of street lamps. The cars he had seen began to move away, probably driven by parents determined that their small daughters shouldn't get wet. They swished past and beyond him, turning right on to the Stewarton Road. Soon the street was as comparatively deserted as before. The dark alley loomed in front.

He left the lights behind. Craig's Wynd they called this narrow, cobbled place. In days gone by it had been the road by which Jenny's forbears had led their horse-drawn carts up into the village. There they had exchanged farm produce for groceries and household goods before returning down the alley and across the ford to Ardcapple.

On either side were the blank rear walls of tenement buildings. His footsteps echoed against them, and he cringed at their loudness.

A shadow moved against the right-hand wall. He stopped. After a time he said: 'Hullo, there!' But the shadow was already gone, utterly silent.

39

At the foot of the alley was Riverside Street, sparsely lit, flanked on its far side by a fence on the bank of the burn. A car passed along it, headlights revealing the figure of a girl in Brownie uniform hurrying towards the old houses near the golf course. The car stopped for a second or two, out of his sight. Then it moved on again, engine revving, gears crackling. The sound and the headlight glare receded into the distance, into the area of the lonely road running between the golf course and the Breckrie.

At the time Alec paid small attention to the behaviour of the car. He was afraid of the dark. He was trying to discipline himself, to subdue and thrust back escaping tendrils of terror. His nerves were becoming raw again, causing a recurrence of his headache. He was possessed by a conviction that evil had come brushing by, an evil spiritual rather than physical. Once, as a boy, he had been possessed in the same way while visiting the Druid cave under Columba's Crag, where, long ago, children had been sacrificed to appease an angry god.

He forced himself to move on, slipping on the cobbles, staggering a little. That he was partly drunk he admitted to himself. But something else was clawing at his senses, something cold and clammy which threatened to obliterate his reason altogether. Shapes stirred and undulated in his mind. They were like parts of a jigsaw puzzle, arranging and rearranging themselves in nightmare patterns.

Almost without being aware of it, he crossed Riverside Street and approached the bridge. But presently the nearness of the bridge impinged on his consciousness. He halted, hesitated, then shied away. There was something about the bridge that reminded him of Elizabeth. He must forget about Elizabeth. If he ignored the bridge,

40

the pictures of Elizabeth might stop crowding in. Ignore the bridge, destroy the pictures.

He shambled along the street. Bordering the dark road beyond the street he found a fence and climbed it. Get away from the bridge. Choose a happier place to walk in. The golf course was a happier place. There he and Willie had laughed and relived adventure only that afternoon. There he had met a girl with dark red hair who was nothing like Elizabeth.

But the pictures kept recurring.

He caught pictures of bright brown hair and recognised its scent as he buried his face in it. He saw an arm and a body gleaming white, and Elizabeth's eyes close to his own, rolling as he pandered to her lust.

The eyes were soft and languorous, dark blue like gentians. Next moment the eyes were no longer soft but filled with amused contempt, and 'love like a bird in flight flew out by the open door'.

Then his hands were sliding along her bare arms and shoulders, reaching for her throat, the slender white throat of Elizabeth the temptress, who had made a fool of him and sacrificed his manhood to a passing fancy.

Trembling, he came to himself again.

His waterproof was sodden with the persistent rain. His trouser-legs were wet, his shoes heavy with mud. Whins and thick bushes clung to his legs and scratched his ankles. He tried to avoid them, to turn back, but they were reluctant to let him go.

Quite close, in the confusion of wet blackness at the centre of the Knowe, somebody screamed. He *thought* somebody screamed.

This time he did turn back. He attempted to run, like a startled animal. But he tripped and stumbled and thudded down among the whins. He lay still, and there

41

was silence, except for the sough of the wind and the thin patter of the rain.

Had the scream occurred in his imagination? Or was it, in fact, the *memory* of a scream?

It was so dark, so dark above and so dark within. His hands were scratched. Wet from the undergrowth seeped through his trousers and chilled his knees.

He struggled to rise, but something clutched at his chest and held him down. He wrenched himself up, and two of the buttons on his waterproof were torn off by the protruding branch of a whin. It sagged open. Rain spattered on his collar and shirt, but he was so thankful to be free that he scarcely noticed.

And now, armed with the knowledge of freedom, he faced the truth. He had made a mistake. There was no happiness on the golf course. Evil dogged him wherever he went.

It was the drink. That was the main cause of the trouble. It wasn't all the foul torture of illness. One normal word, one normal hand on his cheek and he was certain he could be calm and self-possessed again. Here in the dark and in the rain nothing was normal. He must escape. He must find someone who would help him to escape.

He began to run back towards the fence. There was a rustling and a crackling in the whins behind him. Only the wind, only the wind, he told himself. He didn't pause. He didn't look back.

The normal word could be Peter's, or it could be Willie's. But both were so remote, Peter in Kilcolum House a mile away, Willie with his mother in the cottage at the entrance to the golf course, even farther away. There was the Manse, with Kate Thomson, wise and strong and beautiful, waiting inside. But to reach the

42

Manse he would have to go back through the village, and that was unthinkable. No casual pedestrian must see him in a state like this. Let the side down, let the Frasers down? Not on your life.

He climbed the fence and came close to the bridge again. Invisible below, the Breckrie flowed and muttered gently, and he looked across and in the dark imagined that he saw a silvery field of barley on the other side. He ran for the bridge. His shoes clattered on the wooden steps. Arms outstretched, fingers touching the twin handrails. He stumbled across and down on to the track beyond.

A light shone in the cottage window. Was Virginia Semple working at her typewriter, awaiting the return of her young husband from the Fraser Arms? He ran past it, eyes focussed on the other light, a hundred yards ahead.

The light above the front door of Ardcapple was a sign of succour, of rescue. He knew now it was Jenny he wanted: Jenny who had the power to soothe him and warm him against her body, Jenny who had told nobody of their night together in the barley and would never tell of his drunken panic now.

Panting, almost blinded by pain, he opened the gate and stumbled along the garden path and hammered with his fist at the door. He hammered again, and inside there was a flutter of footsteps. The door opened.

She stood in the light from the porch, still wearing the short red skirt. But her anorak was off, revealing a yellow jumper, and her hair without the headscarf was loose and soft.

'Alec!' she said, almost soundlessly, and her eyes were wide.

He fell on his knees. He clutched her to him, hiding

his head against her thighs. 'I'm afraid, Jenny! I'm afraid!'

She was shocked, unable to understand. But instinctively she put an arm about him and stroked his wet, dishevelled hair with her free hand.

Archie Craig was a big man, bordering sixty yet still burly and erect. Faintly, in a blur of relief and returning stability, Alec heard the clump of his feet approaching, caught a glimpse of his checked sports jacket as he came to investigate the commotion.

Trembling, Jenny whispered: 'It's Alec Fraser, Dad. He's ill.'

Alec stirred and looked up. Jenny's presence and her father's comfortable bulk began to effect a cure. He rose to his feet, swaying a little. He caught Jenny's hand and held on to it. With increasing optimism he realised that once again the pain was receding.

'I'm sorry, Mr Craig. I had a drink or two in the hotel with Dan Sillars and Dr Young. On my way home I got lost on the golf course. I—I saw your light and . . .'

'Glad to be of help, Alec.' The big farmer was wary of too much talk, too much emotion. His stout, bristling cheeks broadened in a smile. 'Come in and say hullo to the missus.'

Purposefully, he led the way through the hall and into the living-room.

Mrs Craig was small and neat, with prematurely grey hair expertly permed. 'Alec Fraser!' she cried, putting down her knitting and rising from the sofa. 'How lovely to see you!'

She had heard every word exchanged in the porch and was well aware of her daughter's shock and embarrassment, but no flicker of curiosity betrayed her knowledge. She bustled round, shaking Alec's hand, instructing her husband to take his waterproof, gesturing to Jenny to plump up the cushions on an armchair.

'Such horrible weather, Alec! So changeable. No wonder you got caught out in it. What a welcome on your first day in Kilcolum! Now, please sit down and make yourself comfortable. Your trouser-legs will soon dry by the fire. And do take your shoes off. That's it. I'm sure they're damp. Here are Archie's slippers: he'll be glad to lend them to you. There, a perfect fit. Now you can relax, and Archie will get you a dram . . .'

'No drams, please. I—I've had enough.'

'Then you'll drink a cup of tea? No, no, you're not to think it's any bother. We were just about to have one ourselves.'

'Thank you, Mrs Craig. You're very kind, but . . .'

With quick understanding Jenny said: 'I'll phone the Big House if you like? Tell Meg you'll be late?'

'If you would, Jenny.'

He'd been watching her eyes, searching them for a signal in answer to his need. But they remained quick with alarm and wonder; the old tenderness was still missing.

'Well, that's splendid,' said Mrs Craig, following her daughter to the door. 'I'll bring the tea in a jiffy. Look after your guest, Archie.'

They sat on opposite sides of the fire. Both men were embarrassed, searching for friendly, conventional words. But the situation was unconventional; ordinary words were hard to utter.

Alec said: 'I was ill. A kind of nervous breakdown.'

'So we heard. Could happen to anyone.'

'Trouble is, I've been on pills. Anti-depressants. I don't expect they mix too well with whisky.'

45

'Not to worry, Alec. You may have felt bad out there, but you're fine now.'

'I know. It's all so crazy. I meant to take the short-cut home, past Ardcapple, but when I came to the bridge —well, I was suddenly scared stiff. Peter told me this afternoon about Nancy MacKay, and I think the way she died must have been at the back of my mind. Anyway, I ran away from the bridge and climbed the fence into the golf course. Next thing I knew I was scrambling about on the Whinny Knowe. I fell, and a branch of whin ripped the buttons off my coat. Look at my hands. Look at my trouser-legs, stiff with prickles. Then I found myself racing back towards the bridge, like a bat out of hell. The odd thing is, as soon as I saw Jenny— as soon as I saw you, Archie—I began to feel better. More like myself.'

The friendly comprehension he had failed to find in Jenny's eyes was evident in her father's.

'That's good, Alec. Shows there's nothing much wrong with you. But what were Dan and the doctor thinking about, filling you up with whisky and letting you start off home by yourself?'

'My own fault. They both offered to drive me back. But I was rude about it and refused. You know how it is. We all had too much.'

'Ay. Best forgotten, the whole business . . .'

Jenny came in. 'I told Meg you'd been at the hotel with Dan and Jimmy—her father and the doctor—and that you'd dropped in to see us on the way home. She understood. Says you're not to stay too late.'

'Thanks, Jenny.'

'Now,' she went on briskly, reminding him for a moment of her mother, 'you need a wash and brush up.'

46

She held out her hand and pulled him to his feet. 'I'll show you the bathroom.'

She had become bright and cheerful, like a nurse talking as an aid to therapy. But as they went through the hall there was no warmth between them.

Alec washed his face and hands. His headache and his panic were almost gone. In their place, however, was a dull knowledge of hope unfulfilled. He had seen a mirage and had rushed towards it. The mirage was still there but as far away as ever.

And yet, as they drank tea in the sitting-room and the talk flowed with casual friendliness, he experienced a taste of the relaxation that had for so long eluded him. Mrs Craig made darting forays into local gossip, bringing him up to date with births, deaths and marriages. Her husband smoked his pipe and between bouts of striking matches offered occasional words of wisdom on the state of agriculture in Kilcolum.

When the tea-things had been cleared away Jenny sat beside Alec on a stool by the fire and prepared to sew new buttons on his waterproof. She seemed smaller and slighter than he remembered. Yet her hair was the same, glossy brown and soft. The curve of her cheek and neck were the same, her skin as delicate as a schoolgirl's. He wanted to touch her, to say or do something that would pierce her armour of restraint and rekindle the love and excitement that had once existed between them.

Then she threaded her needle and the diamonds on her left hand sparkled in the light.

He said: 'What do you teach, Jenny?'

'Anything and everything. Infants,' she said.

'You like it?'

'I like the children.' The words hung in the still warmth around the fireplace.

Mrs Craig said, quickly: 'After the summer holidays Jenny won't be teaching any more. She's getting married.'

He stiffened and glanced at Jenny. She tugged at a tangled thread. She didn't look up, but her face was suddenly flushed and unstable.

'We'll miss her,' said Archie Craig. 'But her mother and I are lucky to have had her for so long. Maybe we'll retire now. There's a house in the village I have my eye on.'

'Who's the lucky man?' There was a blunt edge to Alec's voice.

'Dan Sillars,' she told him.

Mrs Craig's sharp eyes inspected his face. He controlled himself, nodded and said: 'Congratulations.'

She laid the waterproof across her knees, put down the needle and thread. The repair was complete. On the point of saying something, Archie Craig caught his wife's eye and instead began to puff loudly at his pipe and strike more matches.

Jenny looked up at Alec. Her eyes were defiant. This was a new element in her character. When he'd known her as a girl of twenty she'd been warm, eager, generous with emotion.

She said: 'Dan is a good headmaster. A good man, in spite of all his revolutionary ideas.' She smiled with brittle brightness, like an actress at a party. 'He's been very lonely since his first wife died and Meg married your brother.'

The guard-rail of the bridge was splintering. He felt exposed, vulnerable.

She turned her head away. 'Not being an unattached spinster any more, it's quite a thrill,' she said.

'Quite.' He got up. 'I'd better be going, Mrs Craig.'

'Yes. Meg didn't want you to be late.' She ignored his abruptness, smoothing it out with normality. She went on: 'It was good to see you, Alec. You must come again, often.'

'I don't know about good for you. It was good for me.' He managed to smile. 'Whatever came over me tonight Ardcapple has certainly cured it.'

'I'll get the car out,' said Archie Craig, hospitably.

'Nonsense. I can walk.'

'A couple of minutes will do it. You'll offend me if you refuse.'

He had hoped it might be Jenny who would volunteer to drive him home. But the effect of the whisky was wearing off; he was aware of mental and physical exhaustion. He said: 'Well, it's kind of you, Archie, and perhaps in the circumstances ...'

The telephone rang, out in the hall.

'I'll get it.' Jenny's voice was uncertain as she handed him his coat.

She went out.

Confidentially, Mrs Craig said: 'I can see you're surprised at her engagement to Dan. Archie and I were surprised, too, when it happened. Even a little worried. You know, the difference in ages. And recently—well, Alec, haven't you noticed she's changed?'

'Now, Mother'—for once her husband dared to expostulate—'Jenny's old enough to know her own mind.'

'I wonder? She seldom mixes with people. Always such a home bird ...'

She came in from the phone. The painful colour had drained from her cheeks. She looked anxious.

'Kate Thomson, phoning from the Manse. Our local Brown Owl, Alec. Apparently one of her Brownies hasn't reported home after the meeting in the Hall—

49

Mary Allen, who lives in one of the old houses near the golf course. Kate wondered if she might be here.'

'Mary Allen?' said Mrs Craig, sharply.

'That pretty little blonde, only about eight years old. Tom Allen's daughter. He's a joiner with Isaac Semple.'

'Of course. She often comes here to watch the milking!'

'Yes. Her mother's very upset. She's at the Manse now.'

Archie Craig said, gruffly: 'Grace Allen's always upset about something. She's a MacKay, and it's a family failing. I expect Mary's with some pal of hers, at a house where there isn't a phone.'

'That's what Kate Thomson hopes. She and Mrs Allen plan to make a round of all Mary's friends. They're starting off now.'

'Miss Thomson's a sensible girl. More than can be said for the minister at times!' He smiled broadly, then came back to earth. 'Well, Alec, we'd better go,' he said. 'You look a bit tired.'

Alec nodded. Mrs Craig fussed round him at the door.

He met Jenny's eyes. They were questioning, on the brink of fear. But no longer defiant.

5

THE thin rain of the night before had been swept away by a rollicking wind from the west. There was cold sunshine often dimmed by scurrying flotillas of clouds.

Spray burst on the shore, glistening against a blue-patched sky.

That morning Mrs MacKay failed to appear at Kilcolum House.

During breakfast Meg was in a puzzling mood.

She was pleasant enough to Alec, asking him a number of questions about his meeting with her father and the doctor and about his visit to Ardcapple—questions which he answered with an unrevealing and slightly ersatz light-heartedness.

When she spoke to Peter, however, there was an edginess in her manner which betrayed to him that for some reason she was nervous and in need of comfort. He put it down to her disappointment at the non-arrival of her daily help and tried to cheer her up by matching Alec's banter.

When the telephone rang in his office across the hall he half rose to answer it; but she forestalled him, striding towards the door with a sharp admonition that he should sit down and get on with his breakfast.

He shrugged and made a wry face at his brother. 'We'll have to rally round,' he said, lowering his voice. 'Help her out with the chores.'

Alec smiled, reaching for a final piece of toast. 'I'll do that. No need to interrupt your lordly routine on the farm. I'm an expert, remember. Six years' training in a bachelor flat.'

'Now who's kidding? You spent most of the time in foreign hotels, luxuriating on an expense account!'

Meg returned hurriedly, in distress, pushing long hair back from her face. 'Oh, Peter, it was Mrs MacKay. She has to stay and look after her niece, Grace Allen. Grace's daughter Mary, she's missing.'

'What!'

51

'I *knew* there was something wrong this morning. I could feel it. She didn't come home last night after a Brownie meeting. Kate Thomson called in the police after she and Grace had made inquiries at practically every house in the village. But there's still no sign of her, and now Inspector Greenlees is at the Fraser Arms, organising a full-scale search.'

With an odd quietness Peter said: 'I'd better get down there, Alec. Coming?'

'If Meg would like me to stay and help . . .'

'Of course not! It's Mary who needs help. Oh, darling,' she said, putting her arms about her husband, 'I hope you find her!'

They wasted no more time. Collecting two of the hired men who were working in the byre, they drove down to the village in the Land Rover. In the lounge of the Fraser Arms they reported to Inspector Greenlees of the Stewarton Police.

Uniformed, square and solid, Greenlees had a ruddy face packed with flesh like a tightly rolled ham. Showing deference to the laird, who was also a J.P., he said: 'Glad to have your help, Mr Fraser. Yours, too, sir,' he added, inclining his head in Alec's direction. 'We've been through the village with a small tooth-comb. We've investigated the roads and byways, too, but until now, of course, it's been too dark to make anything like an exhaustive search of the countryside. If she'd wandered into the open fields north of the village I reckon somebody would have seen her by this time. So, to begin with at any rate, I've decided to concentrate on the river and the golf course, near her home. We'll be starting in a few minutes, once Sergeant MacKinlay and Constable Reid get that crowd outside into some kind of order.'

It was obvious that unofficially the inspector feared

a tragedy. But when Peter asked if he had any idea what might have happened to the girl his answer was stolidly non-committal.

'None. She left the Hall with the other Brownies at approximately eight o'clock. It was raining, and they separated quickly. One little girl says she saw her running off down Main Street and turning right at the junction. That seems to be the last anybody saw of her.'

Peter rubbed his chin, looking more puzzled and upset than even the circumstances seemed to warrant. 'But the Allens live by the golf course. Surely Mary ought to have turned left into Fisher Row—or continued on through Craig's Wynd—if she meant to go home?'

'That occurred to me, sir.' Greenlees's voice was weighty with wisdom. 'But both Fisher Row and Craig's Wynd are badly lit. Her friends say she was afraid of the dark and always preferred to take the long way round, through the new housing scheme off Stewarton Road and back along Riverside Street where there are lamps.'

'I see. Could she have climbed the fence on Riverside Street, perhaps, then fallen down the bank into the river?'

'It's a possibility.' His voice made it a probability.

'Nasty business. Especially for the parents. Let's hope it doesn't turn out to be as serious as it looks.'

'Amen to that, sir.'

Alec had slept fitfully, in spite of the comfort of his room and the soporific sound of the sea washing against the rocks beneath Columba's Crag. Dreams had interrupted spells of heavy sleep: dreams in which whins and human hands plucked at his body, in which somebody screamed, beyond the horizon of his consciousness. Time and again their ugliness had caused him to wake up sweating, intensely aware of loneliness and loss. Jenny was not for him. Not any more. Neither in body nor in spirit.

To begin with, the freshness of the morning had made him see the events of the night before in saner perspective. Jenny was engaged to Dan Sillars, but she remained his friend and might still offer help if he asked for it. As for the condition that had led to his stupid floundering on the Whinny Knowe and in the Craigs' front porch, he had begun to believe that its root cause had been too much unaccustomed whisky and that basically his convalescence was unaffected.

Now, however, shaken by the news of Mary Allen's disappearance and by the prospect of a police investigation, he was faced by an urgent problem. Should he allow himself to become personally involved in this local mystery? If he did, then the crude implications of his performance on the golf course and at Ardcapple would almost certainly become a talking-point in Kilcolum. How would this affect Jenny? How would it affect Peter and Meg, still unaware of the truth?

Only for a few seconds did he consider hiding what he knew. Then his upbringing and training reasserted themselves. Another human being needed help, perhaps more than he did. He could not deny offering this help, even though it might prove to be irrelevant and costly to himself.

'Inspector,' he said.

'Yes, Mr Fraser?'

'Last night I was with friends, here in the Fraser Arms. We left about eight o'clock. I saw the Brownies coming out of the Hall. Some of them ran off, presumably towards their homes. Others were picked up by two cars.'

Greenlees held up a fleshy hand, like a minister inspired by prayer. 'We have investigated those cars. They

belonged to two business men living in Stewarton Road
—Mr Freeman, the solicitor, and Mr MacPhail, the bank
agent. They gave lifts to a number of children, including
their own. But not to Mary Allen.' The prayer was finished. He lowered his hand. 'Go on, sir,' he said.

'My intention was to take the short-cut home, via
Ardcapple, so I went straight down into Craig's Wynd.
When about half-way through, I noticed a little girl in
Brownie uniform running past along Riverside Street.
Then a car went by, going in the same direction. Towards
the golf course.'

Peter had begun to watch him, curiously intent.

With official calm, Greenlees said: 'Anything further,
Mr Fraser?'

'I wasn't quite myself at the time. Rather too much
to drink.' He was scourging his ego. A tightness in his
forehead threatened a new attack of migraine. He continued: 'My impression is that the car stopped soon after
it passed the foot of the alley and then went on again,
taking the road by the golf course.'

'Did you recognise the little girl?'

'No, Inspector.'

'The car?'

Alec shook his head. 'I'm virtually a stranger in Kilcolum. Anyway, I was busy with my own thoughts. I
can't even tell you what make the car was, though I'm
sure it wasn't a Rover or a Jaguar or anything big like
that.'

'And you'd be too far away to see the number?'

'Yes.'

Greenlees glanced at Peter, who was frowning, then
back at Alec. He camouflaged a feeling of disquiet. He
said: 'This may be useful information, Mr Fraser. Is
there anything else?'

With an almost masochistic desire to unload the remainder of his guilt, Alec was about to mention the scream he thought he'd heard on the Whinny Knowe. Before he could speak, however, a policeman in plain clothes entered briskly by the front door.

Sergeant MacKinlay was narrow-faced and volatile, affecting a modern haircut and long black side-pieces like the young detectives in *Z Cars*. He was the representative in Stewarton of the County CID.

He said: 'Search-party organised, sir. Ready when you are.'

'Right.' At the prospect of action the inspector shed his uneasiness. 'I may have to talk to you again, Mr Fraser. Depends on—well, depends on how things go, doesn't it?'

They went out into the breezy sunshine.

The search-party was made up of more than thirty volunteers, including farmers, farm-workers, shopkeepers, labourers from a builder's yard and tradesmen from Isaac Semple's joinery. Kate Thomson, along with a few housewives and shopgirls, had offered to help, but on the inspector's advice Sergeant MacKinlay had persuaded them that in the meantime their services would not be required.

Alec noticed that Willie the Bomber and Archie Craig were among the crowd, the gravity of the situation reflected in their faces. He saw young Isaac Semple, wearing an open-necked red shirt and scruffy jeans.

Then he became aware of a tall, elderly man with grey side-whiskers talking to the inspector and realised that old Isaac Semple was also a volunteer. The outmoded long black coat, the rusty bowler hat and the equally rusty voice were unmistakable.

Other men who might have been there were absent. But from the talk drifting around he gathered that the minister was with Mrs Allen, doing his best to comfort her; the doctor was attending a confinement at an out-lying farm, and Dan Sillars was at his post in the School, endeavouring to persuade excited and frightened children that this day was the same as any other.

Jenny, thought Alec, would be engaged on the same impossible task of dissimulation.

The party was divided into three sections.

The first, under Constable Reid, who lived in the vill-age, had among its number Archie Craig and young Isaac. It was scheduled to operate in the low-lying Ard-capple fields, which contained several deep ditches and a number of bramble thickets. Though nobody put the idea into words, many remembered it was beside one of those thickets that Archie Craig had found a strangled sheep.

The second section, under Sergeant MacKinlay, was to be responsible for the banks of the river and the river itself. Commander Heathergill, who, though Secretary of the Golf Club, was also a keen fisherman, kept a small boat on the bank near the Ardcapple bridge. This was requisitioned by the police, and the Commander himself took the oars, red-faced, clad in an ancient golf jerkin and an even more ancient deerstalker hat with bright fishing flies stuck in the flaps. MacKinlay leant over the stern, ready to begin dragging with a boathook.

The third section, to which Peter, Alec and old Isaac Semple were attached, was commanded by the inspector, with Willie MacNaughton as his guide and adviser. It was spread out across the golf course, like a line of beaters at a grouse drive.

At a signal from Greenlees, the search began. Men

with bowed heads, probing with sticks, moved slowly over the green land and down along the river in the direction of the sea.

Peter walked next to Willie and the inspector in the centre of the line. Alec stayed close to him. The last thing he wanted was to be in a search-party. He had become convinced that Mary Allen was dead. He felt sick at the thought that he might stumble on her body first, and there was comfort in the nearness of his brother. In any case, his walking companion on the other side was old Isaac, dourly keeping pace, and he was determined to keep his distance, to avoid risking an exchange of words with a man whose views on drunkenness and fornication were so implacable.

As they approached the Whinny Knowe he saw that if he continued in the way he was going he would be forced to trample through its left-hand fringe. Imperceptibly he began to edge leftward even closer to Peter.

Anxiously, Peter glanced across and said: 'What's up, Alec?'

'Nothing. Except that I hate this kind of thing.'

'So do we all. You didn't tell me you had a skinful last night.'

'Much more than a skinful. I'll tell you about it later.'

'Is there something . . .'

Inspector Greenlees's voice boomed out: 'Close in, men. Concentrate on the Knowe.'

Obediently they converged, deserting the fairways on either side. The chill air was filled with crushing, crackling sounds as heavy boots trampled through bushes and whins.

Alec lagged behind, feeling so hot and tired that in

an attempt to achieve coolness he unbuttoned his water-proof and let it flap open.

The place looked different in the daylight. He had no idea where he had tripped and fallen the night before. He tried to forget the humiliating details and to remember instead the fun and excitement of the day Willie and he had crawled in the undergrowth, hiding from his father's wrath. It was somewhere here, on this piece of higher ground, that they'd finally gone to earth, giggling in the shelter of a big rabbit warren watching through waving fronds of bracken as his father threshed about on the perimeter of the Knowe.

Yes, this was the place. Since his boyhood rabbits in their thousands had died of myxamatosis; but the grass-grown ruin of the warren was still plainly discernible. If he looked right he could see the river. The boat manned by Commander Heathergill and Sergeant MacKinlay was approaching the rocky promontory from which, with Willie's help, he'd netted the big fish. If he looked left he could see the red flag on the tenth green flapping in the wind as it had flapped on that day nearly twenty years ago. If he looked in front . . .

Ten yards in front a group of men including the inspector, Willie and old Isaac crouched above something on the ground. Peter stood erect beside them.

At a word from Greenlees, Willie detached himself from the group. He waved his hand. 'All over,' he called to the searchers on the Knowe.

Then, putting two fingers in his mouth, he whistled. To Sergeant MacKinlay on the river and to Constable Reid on the far bank he signalled with beckoning arms an end to the operation. Men began to hurry towards the Knowe.

Moving forward on legs awkward and heavy, Alec

caught a glimpse of small twisted limbs, of a plastic coat gaping and torn, of a Brownie scarf knotted about a child's white throat.

He stopped. This was it. This was what he'd been dreading. He bent down and vomited among the whims.

He was shivering. He saw old Isaac get up from his knees and remove his bowler hat. He heard the rasping voice: 'Find him, Greenlees! Find the maniac who did this, or the folk of Kilcolum will call you cursed!'

It was a nightmare, and this testamental screech was part of it. The scent of wet, mangled foliage made him feel ill again.

He found Willie beside him.

'Alec, what's the trouble?'

'I'm sick. Can you blame me?'

'Nobody's blaming you. It's bloody horrible!' He put an arm about Alec's shoulders, his red moustache flyting in the wind. 'Poor Tom Allen!' he said. 'Poor Grace!'

'Sure. No golf today, Willie.'

'No golf today. Come on, son. Time we got back to the village. Peter's just behind us.'

As had happened so often before, he followed where Willie led.

6

MEN returned to their work, angry and sour.

Dr Jimmy Young delivered a healthy boy, left him and his equally healthy mother in charge of the midwife and then, responding to an urgent telephone call, gunned his cream-coloured Volkswagen down towards the Whinny Knowe. When he arrived he found that a colleague from Stewarton—the police surgeon—was already examining the body, while ambulance men stood by with a stretcher.

He found also that Inspector Greenlees, Sergeant MacKinlay and Constable Reid, reinforced by three constables summoned from the town, were carrying out a methodical search of the area. Greenlees was convinced that the killer, blundering about among the whins, must have left behind some clue to his identity. He was determined to find it.

In a small stone house, only a few hundred yards away, the Rev. Harry Thomson and his sister Kate were engaged on a different kind of duty. They sat with Grace Allen, listening with patient distress to her cries of grief, to her husband's bitter condemnation of an unknown murderer, to the quiet weeping of Mrs MacKay.

Tom Allen said: 'I should have gone to meet her.' He was about forty, thin, bald and dyspeptic. His bony hands, skilful with a saw or chisel, were unable to prevent a tea-cup from rattling loudly as he put it down. 'It was dark,' he said, remembering again. 'And cold and wet. I should have gone to meet her. But I never thought . . .'

'Don't blame yourself, Tom.' The minister wore his working uniform of black coat and clerical collar. His young voice was authoritative. 'Scores of times Mary made the same journey, in the dark and in the daylight. It was chance—an evil chance that no one could have foreseen.'

'Isaac warned us. He was here last night, asking if I could go to the shop this morning a bit earlier than usual. A farmer on the Stewarton Road wanted a five-barred gate made in a hurry. He—he'll have to wait for it now.'

Momentarily Tom Allen had gone back to workaday normality. Now the nightmare overcame him again. He put his elbows on the table and buried his face in his hands. 'Isaac warned us,' he repeated. 'He said Mary shouldn't be going out by herself on a dark night. He said there were wicked men, waiting for a chance. We never heeded him. You know what he's like with his fire and brimstone. But he was right. Grace and I were wrong.'

'You couldn't have foreseen what happened. Neither could Isaac. There's no need to reproach yourself . . .'

'Easy to say, Mr Thomson!' The joiner raised his head. Big hands splayed out on the table. 'By God,' he whimpered in his throat, 'if I find the bastard who did it —if I find him before the police do, I'll kill him!' The hands swept against the cup, overturning it. Tea slopped on the table.

'No, Tom!' The minister was suddenly pale, no longer authoritative. 'You must never think like that. Killing settles nothing.'

Grace Allen was a fresh-faced woman made old and ugly by bereavement. The clatter of the cup unloosed a fresh surge of sorrow.

'Why did I let her join the Brownies?' she wailed. Beyond tears, beyond reason, she turned like a spitting animal on Kate Thomson. 'You persuaded me to let her join. You said it would give her confidence, an only child. You said it would make her happy. Oh, God, why did I listen?'

'I'm sorry, Mrs Allen.' Kate's green suède jacket hung open, and for once her thick red hair was undisciplined. She tried to put herself in the place of an agonised mother and to make allowances. 'But Mary *was* happy. She loved being with the other little girls . . .'

'Why did God take her, not one of them?'

Despite her strength of body and character, Kate was trembling as she put her hand on Grace Allen's arm. 'Sometimes God's purpose is hard to understand.'

'I let her wear the bracelet last night. She found it in a drawer—oh, weeks ago—and always wanted it. I let her wear it last night.'

'Well, that was kind of you. But it can't have any bearing . . .'

'It might have. I've been thinking. I've been thinking and thinking . . .' She broke off, sobbing.

Not even trying to make sense of the confusion in the woman's mind, Kate said: 'I understand. One remembers so many things at a time like this.'

Grace Allen caught her breath. She stared at her visitor. 'Perhaps it's a punishment,' she whispered. 'A judgment on me!'

'For what, Mrs Allen? You've lived a good life . . .'

'That's what you think! You don't know what it's like to be a poor girl in a place like this, hemmed in, watched over, with no pretty clothes to wear. Then a man comes along and offers you excitement and money to spend . . .'

'Mrs Allen! Please don't tell me any more. You might regret it, afterwards. But I do know what you mean. I do know what it's like to be a girl with normal instincts, hemmed in as you say and succumbing to temptation. We all have dark places in our lives, but we conceal them and try to make amends. I cannot believe that God looks into them and wreaks vengeance because of what He finds.'

'Oh, I don't know, Miss Thomson.' The woman started sobbing again. 'I just don't know.'

The day wore on past mid-day.

In the Fraser Arms Alec sat beside his brother at a small table in the lounge. With them were the doctor and Willie MacNaughton. Peter and the doctor were drinking whisky. Willie had asked for an export. Catching Peter's eye, Alec had done the same.

They were waiting for Inspector Greenlees who had asked if he might have a word with the doctor and Alec when he returned to the Fraser Arms at about half-past twelve. Peter and Willie, anxious about Alec's reaction to the finding of the body, had decided to remain with him.

Jimmy Young was saying: 'Greenlees won't commit himself, but it's difficult to escape the obvious conclusion. Apparently old Isaac put it into words on the Whinny Knowe.'

'That there's a maniac at large?' said Peter, grimly direct.

'Yes. Half insane, but cunning, too. Like Kürten, the German mass murderer.'

'I don't believe it, Doctor!' Willie's stout face was mottled, creased with distaste. 'No' in Kilcolum.'

'Has it occurred to you that he may have practised on a sheep, as Kürten did? Now it's a little girl. The next victim could be a grown woman.'

'No' in Kilcolum!' repeated Willie, shaking his head like a punch-drunk boxer.

'Why not in Kilcolum?' The doctor's face was puffy, veined with small red lines. He looked tired, as was only to be expected after an early call to a confinement followed by the emotional strain of examining a murdered child.

Aggressively he went on: 'You're a romantic, Willie. You find it hard to admit that this lovely little country parish can spew up ugliness and unnatural death. But it's filled with people, and people are the same everywhere, in Lisbon and London, Kansas and Kilcolum. By the law of averages, sexual killers are usually found in urban areas which are more thickly inhabited. But it's not impossible that one should operate here. A matter of blind chance. The last Irish Sweep was won by a trapper in the Yukon. The nearest town was three hundred miles away.'

Doggedly, Willie said: 'But we *know* all the folk in Kilcolum. We've known them all our lives . . .'

'That's not true, for a start. You haven't known the minister all that long. Or Commander Heathergill. Or MacPhail, the bank agent. Or myself, if it comes to that.'

'But these are all respectable folk! I mean . . .'

'Kürten was highly respectable, according to his neighbours. At his trial they testified he was a quiet, well-balanced man, tidy in his dress, intelligent and a good worker.'

Willie gave up the argument. He loved life and always thought of its pleasant side. As a well-meaning extrovert, he hated to be reminded that some of its aspects were dark and cruel.

Young Isaac emerged from the cocktail bar to collect the empty glasses, looking pale and even more gaunt than usual. The doctor suggested another drink. Peter and Willie agreed. Alec said he still had a mouthful or two of beer left. He'd rather not have any more.

As young Isaac went to carry out the order, Alec said: 'This Kürten. Who was he?'

65

'Haven't you heard of Peter Kürten?' There was animation in the doctor's pale blue eyes. 'He was the most infamous sex killer of all time, with the possible exception of Jack the Ripper. Fritz Lang made a film about him, with Peter Lorre in the starring role. *M* it was called. An old film now, but the B.B.C. put it on just a few weeks ago.'

Peter said: 'I saw it. One of those essays in pseudo-psychology. Copious tears for the murderer but very few for the victims.'

'Ay,' said Willie. 'I know what you mean.'

Young Isaac came with the drinks. The doctor put a ten-shilling note on the salver. 'Keep the change,' he said.

'Thank you, sir.' Isaac moved away.

'Never mind the film,' Alec said. 'What kind of a man was Kürten in real life?'

Jimmy Young sipped his whisky and shrugged. 'Far more terrible than in the film. At the age of fifteen he had sexual intercourse with a sheep, then stabbed it to death. Sounds unbelievable,' he agreed, aware of Alec's shudder and Willie's involuntary exclamation of horror. 'But it's all carefully documented, and Kürten himself took pride in confirming the facts. Apparently he went on to kill about fifty people, most of them girls and young women. Some he raped and strangled. Others he attacked with an axe and found sexual satisfaction in watching the flow of blood.'

The doctor offered cigarettes, lit one for himself. 'He settled finally in Düsseldorf in 1925,' he said, 'on the surface a sober married man and worthy citizen. Even his wife had no idea of his dreadful double life until in May 1930 he told her about it. She refused to believe him at first, and he had to describe his crimes in detail in

66

order to convince her. Then she went to the police and Kürten was arrested, quite obviously relieved to confess his guilt in public.'

Peter said: 'They guillotined him, didn't they?'

The doctor nodded. 'In July 1931. On the eve of his execution he told Dr Karl Berg, a psychiatrist, that he hoped he'd hear the sound of his own blood running into the basket, because that would give him intense pleasure.'

Willie looked into his still untasted glass of beer, as if he loathed the sight of it. 'God!' he said. 'That kind o' thing is no' human.'

Peter said: 'He was mad, of course.'

But the doctor shook his head. 'The German judges ruled that he was sane. Today he'd probably be called a chronic psychopath and sent for treatment to an institution.'

Alec saw tall gates opening. As he was dragged inside he heard them clanging shut behind him.

At about twenty to one Inspector Greenlees and Sergeant MacKinlay returned from the Whinny Knowe. Greenlees was hot and clearly under strain. His face had the same puffy look as the doctor's. MacKinlay's ebullience smouldered, threatening to flash into anger. It was the first time he had dealt with the murder of a child.

The manager of the hotel had put a sitting-room at the disposal of the police. They saw Jimmy Young there alone, but the interview lasted only a few minutes. Then the doctor hurried off to have lunch at home before beginning a postponed round of professional calls in the afternoon.

MacKinlay came into the lounge and said: 'Mr Fraser, please. Mr Alec Fraser.'

'May I accompany my brother?' said Peter, getting up.

'If you wish, sir.' The young detective's glance flickered between the two. 'So far it's just routine.'

Willie said: 'Will you be wanting me, Sergeant?'

'I don't think so.'

Peter said: 'You go home, Willie. I'll look after him.'

'Ay, well . . . Don't forget, Alec, my mother and I will be glad to see you any time.'

'Thanks. I know that.'

The small sitting-room smelt faintly of spirits. The window was closed; a two-barred electric heater glowed in front of an empty grate. Despite such precautions, however, the air was chilly, and Alec was glad he'd kept on his waterproof, though most of the cold, he imagined, was in himself.

He was conscious of rows of books in a glass-fronted bookcase, of an old-fashioned marble clock on a modern mantelpiece, of an ugly flower design on new wallpaper; but his attention was almost exclusively drawn to the inspector, seated bulkily at a large round table spread with papers, notebooks and pens, its polished rosewood surface glinting in the sunshine. The setting reminded him of cruel interviews with doctors and psychiatrists.

MacKinlay sat down on Greenlees's right. Alec and Peter took chairs facing them, which meant they also faced the light.

Through the window behind the policemen Alec could see part of the Main Street, where people huddled in small groups, seeking comfort from the shock of the day's news in furtive talk with their neighbours. A number of children were returning to school after the lunch-break, all accompanied by grim-faced adults.

In the distance he saw the river and the fields of Ardcapple on the other side, where Ayrshire cows were sprinkled about like pieces of white fluff on a green carpet. Far away, in a field belonging to the Home Farm, one of Peter's hired men was finishing the ploughing he had begun the previous day. The tractor moved like a small red beetle.

Peter said: 'Have you found anything, Inspector? Anything pointing to . . .'

'As yet we have no idea who killed Mary Allen, if that's what you mean, sir.' Greenlees's voice was sombrely disciplined. 'But we have found several clues which may be of assistance.' He fingered three buff envelopes on the table. He paused for a second, then, with some deliberation, went on. 'There's one fact you may be glad to hear about, if "glad" is the right word in the circumstances. Mary Allen was *not* sexually assaulted.'

The motionless air in the sitting-room seemed to stir and settle again.

'But—but she was strangled?' said Alec, releasing the words against his will.

Greenlees nodded.

MacKinlay looked up. 'With her Brownie scarf,' he said.

Peter moved in his chair, betraying the fact that in spite of his stolid expression he was almost as uncomfortably tense as his brother. 'But surely that puts a different complexion on the case? Dr Young seemed to infer that the murderer was a sex maniac.'

'Dr Young could be right, of course.' Greenlees was an expert at leaving the options open. 'The murderer may have been interrupted. He may have obtained sexual satisfaction in the act of killing. There are various possibilities. But the girl was not raped. Dr Young and the police surgeon are agreed about that. I've told Mr and Mrs Allen. They seemed to find it—comforting.' He sighed, his uniform creasing against the table-edge.

69

'The fact remains,' said MacKinlay, 'that somebody killed the child, brutally. Before midnight last night, according to the medical evidence.' His eyes were on Alec, pale and cold. 'We'll find him. Don't worry. I just hope we lay hands on him before Tom Allen does. For Tom Allen's sake.'

There was another uneasy silence, out of which the inspector said, heavily: 'Before we began the search this morning, Mr Fraser, you told us something of what you'd seen on your way home last night. Could we now go over it again, please?'

'Of course.'

Some of his fears had lifted. A doubt had occurred concerning the motive for the murder. His knowledge of this was a relief, even a release.

'If you don't mind, sir, Sergeant MacKinlay will take notes.'

He repeated his story, encouraged all the time by Peter's solid watchful presence. He told of the girl he had seen running along Riverside Street, of the car that had passed and stopped and gone on again.

'You are certain the girl was wearing Brownie uniform?'

'Quite certain, Inspector.'

Greenlees nodded. 'I feel sure it was Mary Allen you saw, because none of the other Brownies lived near the golf course. You may have been the last person to see her alive—apart from the murderer, that is.'

A creamery tanker passed on the street outside, its weight causing a tremor in the floor of the room. The driver changed gear. The engine roared and whined as it turned right into Stewarton Road.

'But you can't describe the car?' MacKinlay said.

'I'm sorry. I only caught a glimpse of it.'

70

The sergeant stopped writing and thrust his pen towards Alec's face. 'Was it noisy, do you remember? Or was the engine quiet?'

Alec furrowed his forehead. 'It must have been fairly noisy or I don't believe I should have got so distinct an impression that it stopped and started again.'

'Something in that,' acknowledged MacKinlay, grudgingly. He made a note, then looked up again. 'You have admitted you were slightly under the influence at the time. Are you sure there was a car at all?'

'Oh, yes. In my own mind.'

'Then you must have noticed *something* about it?'

'It was medium-sized. Not a big one. Somehow or other it seemed—familiar.'

'Familiar?'

'Well, you know—so many cars are alike.'

'What colour was it?'

'I'm not certain.'

'Dark or pale?'

'Pale, I think.'

'You only *think* ...'

'Look, Sergeant, my brother has been ill,' interrupted Peter, harshly. 'He may have had too much to drink last night, but when he says he saw a car you can take it there *was* a car, even though he can't describe it in detail. He's not an alcoholic or a drug addict, living in a world of fantasy.'

'Quite so, sir,' replied MacKinlay, but his tone was neither entirely convinced nor even entirely respectful.

Peter gave him a hard magisterial look, then turned to the inspector. 'Talking about cars,' he said, 'there's a rumour you found fresh tyre-tracks on the roadway by the golf course fence. Where a car might have parked during the night. Is this true?'

'It's true,' said Greenlees, without enthusiasm. 'Un-
fortunately, before we could rope them off, they were
almost obliterated by the tyre-tracks of the ambulance
and the police doctor's car. Dr Young's Volkswagen
was involved as well. The ground was extremely soft
after last night's rain, and vehicles were warned off only
after a good deal of damage had been done.'

'You said *almost* all the tracks were obliterated?'

'Yes. A few of the original impressions may still be
decipherable, and my men are working on that now.
But even though they are successful this may not help us
much. Cars often stop at that particular point to watch
the golf.'

It seemed to both Peter and Alec that the inspector
had become less than frank. His eyes were hooded, his
hands fidgeted with the envelopes on the table.

The sergeant, too, was bent over his notes, drumming
on strong front teeth with the barrel of his pen.

Presently he put an end to his drumming. He said:
'Time we got back to Mr Alec Fraser's statement, sir.'

'Indeed, indeed.' Greenlees raised his praying hand,
coughing a little to conceal his resentment at being taught
his duty by the CID man. He felt perfectly capable of
conducting the investigation in his own canny way, but
his superiors had great faith in MacKinlay's brash
methods, and in any case there was no point in antagon-
ising a colleague at this stage. He coughed again and
went on: 'You heard the car receding into the distance,
Mr Fraser. What did you do then?'

This was the critical question. Alec had been waiting
for it.

Earlier in the day, had it been put to him, he would
have answered at once, glad of an opportunity to unburden the whole sorry tale of his guilt. Now his mood

72

had changed. If he admitted his mad cavorting on the Whinny Knowe, he would immediately come under suspicion. Peter and Meg would be hurt and upset. So would Jenny and her parents. Innocent and unable to protest, they would all be dragged at his coat-tails into the morass of a police inquiry. Meg was expecting a baby, Jenny busy with preparations for her wedding. It would be cruel to involve them in his murky affairs.

And yet, not only as a journalist, but also as a man, he had a natural instinct to tell the truth. It occurred to him in a flash of insight that in the end it might be better if he did, especially for Jenny's sake. He had told the Craigs about his visit to the golf course; they had seen the whin prickles on his clothes; Jenny had repaired his waterproof. If he told the truth now they would be relieved of trying to cover up for him.

He noticed Greenlees looking at the buttons on his coat. He made up his mind and said: 'What did I do then, Inspector? It's a curious story.'

'Well?'

'As I approached the Ardcapple bridge I was suddenly afraid. The drink and the dark and the old scandal about Nancy MacKay's suicide—I expect they all had a bearing on my state of mind. Anyway, I shied off, blundered down the road and climbed the fence on to the golf course. Eventually I found myself on the Whinny Knowe. I thought I heard a scream but put it down to my imagination. I fell, and the branch of a whin caught in my waterproof. As I got up to run away, two buttons were torn off. Then I went to Ardcapple Farm. The Craigs are old friends. Mrs Craig gave me tea, and Jenny put new buttons on my coat. After a time I sobered up and Archie Craig ran me home in his car.'

Peter was watching him with a mixture of astonish-

73

ment and bleak anxiety. MacKinlay's pen sped to a stop. A sidelong quiver of his wide mouth could have been evidence of triumph.

Greenlees's expression had scarcely changed. His manner remained disciplined as he said: 'I'm glad you've been so frank with us, Mr Fraser. I noticed that two of the buttons on your waterproof were slightly smaller than the rest and had been sewn on recently with different thread. It was worrying me.'

'Worrying you?'

'Yes.' He took one of the buff envelopes and shook it open. Two buttons fell, rattling on the table. 'I found these on the Whinny Knowe this morning. It worried me that they matched the other buttons on your coat. But now that you've explained—well, it solves the mystery, doesn't it?'

'Alec,' said Peter, abruptly, 'why didn't you tell me about this last night?'

'Meg was with us until you ordered me to bed. I was afraid she might be shocked. I was afraid it might be bad for her—in her condition, I mean.'

MacKinlay sniffed and cleared his throat, like an actor preparing to go on stage. He fixed Alec with a sceptical eye and said: 'What's this about a scream? Did you hear one, or didn't you?'

'At the time I thought I had imagined it. Now I'm not so sure.'

'Because of the murder?'

'Yes.'

'There's nothing further you want to tell us?'

'Nothing. I've told you everything I know.'

Peter said: 'Inspector, what else did you discover on the Whinny Knowe?'

Greenlees raised and lowered burly shoulders. 'This

74

and that,' he said. His attitude to Peter as a laird and local magistrate had changed. Candour had been replaced by professional caution.

Peter waited. The silence grew sinister.

After a while he straightened his back and said: 'May we go now?'

Greenless nodded. 'That will be all.'

'In the meantime,' added MacKinlay, as they got to their feet.

7

MEG had their lunch ready. Afterwards as they washed dishes in the kitchen, she said she was going down to the village to see if she could help the Allens.

'Or Mrs MacKay,' she added. 'She's been with Grace all morning, and her own house will be neglected. I could tidy up for her, prepare a meal.'

'Darling, are you sure it's wise?' Peter fussed about her. 'I know you're quite strong and fit, but . . .'

'Don't be Victorian, darling.' They were concerned only with each other, almost completely unaware of Alec busy with a cloth at the drying-board. 'I'd feel much worse left here all alone, *thinking* about things.'

'I know. It must have been horrible for you this morning, while we were away. Tell you what. I'd like a word with Isaac Semple about that trailer he's building for me. I'll run you to the village, call back for you later.'

'I could easily walk home, darling. It's not far.'

Peter said: 'After listening to Jimmy Young's lecture about Kürten I'm not going to let you wander about the countryside alone. Not even in daylight.'

She stood on tip-toe and kissed him, her long hair tangling about his face. 'It's a date, then. I keep being selfish and forgetting about junior. But Jimmy's all wrong about a maniac, I'm sure. If anybody in Kilcolum had maniacal tendencies we'd have known about it years ago.'

Peter nodded, concealing doubt. 'I'm inclined to agree with you, darling. Anyway, better not take any risks. If only for junior's sake, as you say.' His arm tightened about her shoulders.

She snuggled close to him, then moved away. 'Right. I'll go and get ready.' At the door she paused, untying her flowered apron. 'Oh, I almost forgot. I had a phone call from Dad at his lunch hour. He's coming over some time tonight, bringing Jenny.'

'Fine. We need a tonic at a time like this, and Dan will provide the strychnine!' As she went out, laughing, he turned and noticed Alec behind him. 'Meg's a real game 'un,' he said. Then, almost guiltily: 'Look, how about coming with us? I don't want to leave you alone either.'

There was constraint between them. The events of the morning, culminating in his interview with Greenlees and MacKinlay, had caused in Alec a kind of numb despair. He knew that both Peter and the police were suspicious of his actions on the previous night. Worse than that, his mind was so confused he'd begun to be suspicious of them himself. He wanted to blurt out his fears to his brother, but there was something odd about Peter today, a kind of wariness that puzzled him.

He said: 'I need fresh air and exercise. I think I'll try a hike to Columba's Crag.'

'Are you sure . . .'

76

'Don't worry, Peter. No whisky in the Druid's Cave.'

He saw them off in the Land Rover. The afternoon was bright, and the fresh wind of the morning was dying away. He put on an old brown anorak which had accompanied him on many assignments abroad and set out across the fields.

He felt tired and drained of energy but forced himself to move briskly, calculating that physical exertion might keep his nerves in control. That day he had deliberately avoided taking a tranquilliser. Now, attacked by forebodings, he was beginning to wonder if this had been a mistake. As yet, however, no positive migraine had developed.

Waves that a few hours ago had showered spray on the rocks were now long and heavy, booming solidly against the shore. The sound had a lulling quality. He looked across the Channel and saw the round blue hills of Antrim lying quiet and serene on the horizon.

Columba's Crag was a bluff of turf-happed sandstone, towering above the sea. Archaeologists had found the remains of a sixth-century cell or chapel on its summit, reinforcing the legend that it was here the Irish saint had built his first church in Scotland. Beneath the Crag, in a grassy hollow on its seaward side, prehistoric tides had excavated a small cave about ten feet high. Inside this cave was a rude stone altar pitted with cup-marks. Obviously Druidic in origin, it bore out the theory of Church historians that St Columba nearly always erected his churches on Druidic sites, such as Iona, building the new faith of Christianity on the foundation of a far more ancient belief.

Alec stood on top of the Crag and let the wind flow gently around him. Picking his way among the irregular, only half-healed scars of the archaeologists' dig,

77

he moved to the edge of the bluff. He looked down and saw the ground falling steeply to a confusion of bushes, which, as he knew, concealed a sheer drop of a hundred feet to the rocky shore. Beneath him seagulls wheeled and mewed, like sad white spirits against the blue.

He was tempted to jump and end it all, to obliterate his doubts and fears concerning Mary Allen. He closed his eyes and the feeling passed. He reviled himself for cowardice. Old Columba, 'strong in stature, voice and spirit', would never have allowed himself such thoughts. Evil had to be exorcised in a positive way. Negative solutions were out.

He went slowly downhill and by way of the western machair-land came to the cave below. Here it was quiet and warm in the shelter of the bluff. At the cave-mouth he sat on a boulder which had fallen from the Crag and now lay half-embedded in the green turf. Lighting a cigarette, he ventured at last to consider his position in regard to the murder. The numbness lifted from his nerves. He began to tremble.

On the shore to his left a piece of driftwood snapped as somebody stepped on it. He looked up and saw Kate Thomson She was already within twenty yards of him, rounding the bluff along its eastern flank.

He got up quickly, throwing away his cigarette. She wore a short skirt of mottled green tweed and a jacket of the same material over a white polo-necked jumper. Her hair was blown about, glinting like dark red wine in the sunshine.

She came and stood close to him, her head not much higher than his shoulders. 'I called at the house to see Meg, hoping to arrange for you all to come to the Manse some evening this week. But the place was deserted, and one of the hired men told me she and Peter had gone to the village. He also said he'd seen you striding off in this direction. I felt like some fresh air, so I decided to try and track you down.'

She smiled at him with the frankness of a schoolgirl expecting praise for her enterprise. There was no wariness in her eyes. Her interest in him was uninhibited. He had a sense of relief, as if suddenly absolved from the necessity of playing a part. The only other person in Kilcolum who had the same effect on him was Willie.

He said: 'That was kind of you. As a matter of fact, I've been feeling rather low and in need of company.'

'I thought as much. So have I, if you want to know. Harry and I were at the Allens' all morning. Poor souls! You can imagine what it was like.'

'Yes. Sometimes I wonder how a clergyman copes. Or a clergyman's sister.'

She gave him a small smile and said: 'Could I have a cigarette, d'you think?'

'Of course. I'm sorry, Miss Thomson.' He brought out his case.

She accepted a light and sat on the boulder, the hem of her skirt sliding high above her knees. 'Thanks,' she said. 'Oh, and by the way, everybody in Kilcolum calls me Kate.'

He sat down beside her and smiled. 'I can imagine! Miss Thomson sounds a bit prim and prissy, a bit schoolmarmish, and you don't look in the least like that.'

'Are all schoolmarms prim and prissy?'

She was being coy about her own former job as a teacher. But he missed his cue and thought at once of Jenny: Jenny as she had been and Jenny as she was. A bleakness of loss touched his heart.

'Not all,' he said.

79

She detected sadness in his voice and with quick intuition understood. She wasn't a woman for nothing, listening with interest to the gossip of parishioners about old flames and new allegiances.

She put her elbows on her knees, flicked ash from her cigarette. 'I know how much you were looking forward to coming home. I'm sorry it turned out to be so—so unhappy.'

The bleakness lifted. His sense of relief returned. He found the dam-wall of his emotions beginning to crumble.

'Thank you,' he said. He took a deep drag of smoke, exhaled it quickly and added: 'You don't know how unhappy.' His hands were unsteady.

She said: 'Tell me, Alec.' She smiled encouragement, then lightly touched his arm. 'You don't mind if I call you Alec?'

He shook his head.

For the past twenty-four hours he had wanted to tell someone about Elizabeth, about the aftermath of their hectic summer. For the past six hours, since news of the local tragedy had broken, he had wanted to tell someone about his fears concerning the death of Mary Allen. In general the people of Kilcolum had been aloof. Peter and Jenny had been kind but hazily remote, worried about him a little but more preoccupied with their own affairs. Willie the Bomber, Dan Sillars and Archie Craig, all cheerfully extrovert, had so far failed to understand he might have problems a good deal more complicated than their own. Now Kate Thomson, a stranger, a girl he scarcely knew, was offering him unconditional sympathy and a chance to unburden his guilt. She was cool, honest, willing to be involved, like someone he had known all his life.

'Can you bear to listen to a confession?' he said.

'I can bear it.' She glanced across and saw how pale he had become. 'But don't tell me anything that might embarrass you later on.'

'I'd rather you knew. I don't know why, Kate, but— I trust you.'

'Now it's my turn to say thank you.'

The air was tangy with the salt scent of the sea and the sea-wrack. The sun was warm. Above them gulls flew and rested on the Crag and flew again, uttering their complaints. He began to talk.

She listened, making no comments. But as he talked, every change in his mood from joy to agony, from fear to self-distrust, was mirrored in her face.

'Elizabeth Andrews. She was an actress: you must have heard of her. We met in Paris, where she was doing cabaret. I fell in love, violently. It was a kind of mental and physical agony to be apart from her. She said her career came before marriage. I accepted that, and for a time we lived together, first in a Paris hotel, then in a flat in London.'

He offered her another cigarette. She shook her head. He lit one for himself.

'In London she introduced me to—to her gang, as she called them. They lived fast and expensively. When they were tired from lack of sleep they took pills. I did, too, and through June and part of July I thought I was happy.'

He looked up at the sun and out across the sea.

'I forgot what this was like,' he said. 'I found peace in drugs and in loving Elizabeth. Then my paper sent me to Brussels—a Common Market Conference—and when I came back in early August I sensed that Elizabeth had fallen for somebody else. She didn't deny it. He was—

and is—a singer with a pop group. Long black hair and a cruel mouth, diamonds on his fingers. She still allowed me to sleep with her, but there was no more love. My nerves began to go haywire. At one stage I tried to break with the drugs. I even tried to break with Elizabeth. But I was hooked, both ways. She knew it.'

He threw away his cigarette, half-smoked. At once he lit another. She sat motionless, elbows on knees, chin in hands. She didn't look at him.

He inhaled smoke deeply, coughed and went on: 'She began to laugh at me, keep me waiting for love. Sometimes I had to do without it. Sometimes I didn't, when her own desire became too strong. She was in a West End play called *Clodhopper Country*. She said I was a clodhopper. She'd compare my love-making with her singer's. "You've lost the art," she'd tell me. "Call yourself sophisticated? Don't make me laugh!"'

Kate felt a shiver of disgust crawling in the muscles of her back. She resisted it, killed it. She knew more than Alec realised about this kind of situation.

He hunched his shoulders and went on: 'One night I got drunk at a party. She was there, too. I took her home. I'd been on pills, so you can imagine the state I was in. We went to bed. I think she was a little scared of me, because at the party I'd tried to assault her singer and had to be dragged away from him.'

He paused and shook his head, slowly.

'Kate,' he said, 'this is the worst part. I began to make love to her. She resisted. She said she felt ill. She was panting in a strange kind of way, but I thought she was putting on her usual act. I tried again. Again she resisted. I was angry and frustrated. I caught her and shook her, and then I may have passed out, though I seem to remember my hands on her body, then on her arms, then on her throat.'

A whimper of sound came from him, as if he were being physically hurt. He put a hand to his forehead.

'I came to my senses. It was dark. Elizabeth lay quiet beside me. I put on the bedlight. It was nearly four o'clock in the morning, and she was dead.'

Two seagulls began squabbling for a scrap of offal on the shore. Neither Kate nor Alec heard them.

He said: 'I called her doctor and the police. I told them I thought I might have killed her. They didn't believe me. They said she hadn't been strangled, as I— as I'd feared. The doctor had known for some time that she had a heart condition. Said he'd been expecting something like this to happen, and after consultation with the police surgeon certified her death as due to heart failure. There was an inquest. The verdict went strictly by the medical evidence. I was absolved from all blame.'

At last Kate ventured to speak. 'Then you allowed your guilt complex to build up? You had a nervous breakdown?'

'Yes. I went to hospital. The doctors taught me how to live without addictive drugs. They tried to get me to talk about Elizabeth, and I did talk a little and it helped. But I've never told anybody the whole truth until now.'

A small gust of wind whined across the summit of the Crag.

Without tone and without expression she said: 'Are you still hooked on Elizabeth?'

He seemed not to understand at first. Then he rubbed his forehead, as if trying to smooth out the furrows. 'Not on Elizabeth,' he said. 'On the feeling that I may have killed her. I thought I was getting rid of it, until

83

yesterday. Almost as soon as I got home things began to crop up which brought it back. Finally, there was last night.'

He looked at her. She was terrified of what he was going to say, but in his eyes she saw nothing but pain and perplexity. Her terror faded.

'Go on. Don't stop now.' Her voice was hard, high-pitched.

He told her, repeating in detail the statement he had made to Inspector Greenlees. 'What worries me,' he said, struggling for resolution, 'is that I may have had a black-out on my way to the golf course. That before I came to myself on the Whinny Knowe I may have met and killed Mary Allen.'

It was out at last. He felt like weeping.

She stood up, slowly. He got to his feet.

She faced him, green eyes blazing. 'Don't be a fool! Don't be a maudlin damned fool!'

If she had slapped his face the result couldn't have been more salutary. His legs felt weak. He stumbled back a little.

'I—I felt I had no one else to confide in. Perhaps it was unfair of me to pick on you. I'm sorry . . .'

'That's your trouble, Alec. You're always being sorry, particularly for yourself.'

'But—put yourself in my place . . .'

She brushed his plea aside. 'You had a raw deal, as they say. But you didn't kill Elizabeth. The law and the doctors proved it. And I *know* you didn't kill Mary Allen.'

'How can you know?'

She hesitated, momentarily embarrassed. Then, almost angrily, she said: 'Please credit me with some adult in-telligence and sensitivity. If you were a murderer I'd de-

84

tect it now, looking into your eyes. All I can see there is self-pity and fear.'

She was physically small beside him; but for the time being his whole world was filled by her.

She went on: 'You've cast yourself in the role of a maniac who at regular intervals is possessed by the urge to kill. You've done this because you feel guilty and are determined to punish yourself.' She saw how each lash of her tongue was hurting him and felt compassion. 'Oh, I know, Alec. You've had a hell of a time. That—that woman. The drugs. The breakdown. And now all this, in Kilcolum, where you expected to find peace. Believe me, I know how you must feel. But you're not fitted for the part of a—of a murderer. You're being ridiculous, juvenile, like a spoilt child wailing for a mother who isn't there.'

She paused, gulping for breath. Her cheeks had lost their colour. Her hands were clenched.

Alec stared at her. His desire to weep was draining from him, allowing anger to take its place. Sordid memories were being burnt away by the fire of her denunciation.

Grimly he said: 'You're probably right.'

'Of course I'm right.' She forced herself not to spare him. 'You were brought up here in Kilcolum, in a warm and uncomplicated community which you understood, which understood you, because you're a Fraser, with a pedigree as long as my arm. You did well at the University. You did well as a newspaperman. Rewards came easy. Then you met this woman and encountered a kind of life you didn't understand. You thought you could cope with sophistication but you couldn't, because basically, in spite of all your travels and in spite of your brilliance as a foreign correspondent, you're still a simple countryman. Maybe that's the secret of your professional success: an ability to observe events from the standpoint of uncommitted innocence. But it's also the secret of your guilt complex. You've betrayed your innocence and are looking for revenge. But you must grow up, Alec. We're all sinners. We all betray our innocence. You must grow up and face the facts of evil, instead of trying to shelter from them behind a puritan conscience. Other people have felt guilt. They've learnt to live with it.'

He saw tears in her eyes, and his anger was tempered by concern for her. He suspected that her incisive words concealed a personal unhappiness. She was trying to help him by reopening old wounds within herself.

'Kate,' he said, 'I . . .'

'Wait!'

She blinked; her body stiffened even more. An eddy of wind invaded the sheltered hollow in the Crag, stirring her hair. Her hands remained by her sides.

'Think back, Alec.' Her voice was quieter, more intense. 'Think back to last night. Did you really have a blackout between the time you ran away from the bridge and the time you found yourself on the Whinny Knowe? Or were you just so miserable that you've made up your mind not to remember?'

He took a quick breath. He was about to reply when she interrupted him again.

'Think carefully,' she said. 'Don't be afraid to hurt yourself. Can you honestly say you don't remember? Can you honestly say you were lost to reality for so long that you had time to kill a little girl and conceal her body on the Whinny Knowe?'

The cruel questions shocked him. He took a step towards her and tentatively held out his hands. She ignored them.

'When you face facts, Alec, you do it on your own.' The tears were there again. 'This is a hard world, and unless you come to terms with yourself, no one is all that ready to come to terms with you.' Her lower lip trembled. Emotion surged between them. 'Afterwards,' she conceded, 'well, afterwards people on the whole are kind.'

He faced the memories. The pictures that had flickered across the screen of his brain—pictures of Nancy MacKay, of Jenny, of Elizabeth—they all came back to him. He related them to the bridge and to places on the riverside and on the golf course.

He looked straightly at Kate and said: 'I can remember. I didn't have a complete blackout. I couldn't possibly have killed Mary Allen.'

She sat down on the boulder, put her hands to her face and began to cry. For the first time in months he forgot about himself. He knelt in front of her. This time he didn't ask that she should take his hands. He took hers and held them and caressed them and made her look at him. She struggled to stop crying.

He said: 'You had to face reality, too?'

She nodded, distrusting speech.

'Would you like to tell me?'

'Not now.' She pulled her hands away, took a handkerchief from her sleeve and wiped her eyes. 'Your problem is more serious. I met Willie MacNaughton in the village, and he told me the police suspect you. More accurately, Sergeant MacKinlay suspects you: the inspector is more discreet. Willie also told me the kind of mood you were in, so when I got the chance I decided to try and help.'

'You have helped.' He smiled. 'My father used to

87

wield a belt with great efficiency. But now, this afternoon —well, I've never had a metaphorical belt laid on to such purpose in my life!'

She smiled, too. 'It seemed the only way. You were down, Alec. Now you must start fighting back.'

'Fighting back?'

'Yes. Like the innocent man that you are. One way would be to start looking at Mary Allen's murder more objectively. Assist the police, if necessary, to find the murderer.'

He stood up, helped her to her feet. There was a strange thought in his mind. In a way, apart from her hair, she looked like Jenny. His physical response to her nearness was as quick and strong as ever it had been to Jenny's. But he realised now that Jenny could never match this girl's strength of will and purpose. It occurred to him that when Dan Sillars married Jenny he would find life much easier and simpler than any man who married Kate.

She said: 'I'll have to get back now. Harry will want his tea earlier than usual. There's a service in the church at half-past six.'

'For Mary Allen?'

'Yes. Her parents want it. The whole village is coming.'

'Will you be there?'

'Yes.'

They moved away, out into the wind, turning their backs on the cave and the sacrificial altar. In the distance tea-time smoke was beginning to plume from village chimneys.

'So will I,' said Alec.

8

A T about six o'clock that evening a call came to the
Fraser Arms from Scotland Yard. MacKinlay answered it. A minute or two later he returned to the sitting-room where Inspector Greenlees, at the table, was
frowning over a pile of reports and statements.

He said: 'The rumours in the village weren't so far
wrong, sir. Alec Fraser was living with Elizabeth
Andrews. She died more or less in his arms in the
early morning of August the fourteenth last year. The
verdict at the inquest was heart failure, but it seems
that at the time Fraser behaved in rather a peculiar
way.'

'How d'you mean peculiar?'

'He tried to tell the police he'd strangled her.'

'Well?'

'In fact there were no marks on her throat, no evidence
of strangling at all. Or even of a struggle. The medical
evidence was quite clear and emphatic. She had heart
disease. Her own doctor expected her to snuff out at any
moment.'

'Then we're not much further forward, are we?'

'I don't know, sir. Whichever way you look at it,
isn't there evidence of mental instability as far as Fraser
is concerned?'

'He was on drugs, his love affair was going sour, he
was on the verge of a nervous breakdown. That's all the
evidence we have. In the same circumstances you'd be
in a pretty unstable condition yourself.'

The inspector was a continual surprise to MacKinlay.
He seemed so slow, so ponderous in thought, so old-

fashioned in his opinions. And yet occasionally he offered comments that were apposite and sharp, revealing much more knowledge of the world than the sergeant gave him credit for. This was one of those times, and MacKinlay reacted more brashly than perhaps he intended.

'What about that old Fraser who was locked up in a looney-bin?'

'What about him? I've heard of Sir James Fraser, of course. A tobacco baron who lived in Glasgow a hundred and fifty years ago, the present laird's uncle five times removed. He took fits and strangled his daughter's lover in one of them.'

'A number of older folk in Kilcolum keep reminding me about him.'

'They keep reminding me about more curious things than that.'

'Then you don't think Sir James is relevant?'

'There's no further history of insanity among the Frasers. I think most families have a skeleton in the cupboard. Haven't the MacKinlays?'

The sergeant bridled a little. 'I couldn't say, sir. Anyway, it's not the MacKinlays we're talking about . . .'

'By the way,' interrupted Greenlees, 'I don't like the term "looney-bin". Insanity is not a subject for casual humour.'

MacKinlay took a deep breath. He caught his temper by the scruff of the neck and disciplined it.

He said: 'To return to the present case, sir. Wouldn't you agree there's a kind of pattern? I mean, Fraser was present when Elizabeth Andrews died. He was present when Mary Allen died.'

'He wasn't present when that sheep died. He was in London.'

'Yes, but haven't we decided the sheep may be irrelevant. Like Sir James Fraser,' he added, with a kind of snarling triumph.

The inspector acknowledged this with a gloomy inclination of his head. 'Go on,' he said, patiently.

'And there's this story he tells. This story about seeing and hearing a car on Riverside Street, then having a kind of blackout because he was scared of the bridge, then finding himself on the Whinny Knowe and hearing a scream. It all sounds phoney to me.'

'That's why I think it may be true. Even a maniac would be unlikely to invent a daft story like that.'

'But if he did have a genuine blackout . . .'

'I know, MacKinlay. It's possible he killed Mary Allen and simply doesn't remember. But not probable. According to the evidence we got an hour ago from the London hospital, he was discharged as cured. In any case, the specialist I spoke to on the telephone was convinced he's no psychopath. I'm prepared to believe that his behaviour was a natural result of overwork, combined with the strain of disappointment in love and with the effect of drugs on a system completely unused to them. It's unlikely that the doctors attending him would fail to discover homicidal tendencies if they were there.'

MacKinlay sat down and smiled with one corner of his mouth. 'I didn't know you were a student of psychology, sir.'

'I'm not.' Greenlees's heavy lids were lowered to hide the distaste in his eyes for the CID man's sense of humour. 'It's just that I've learnt to respect the opinions of experts. Incidentally, it's not psychology we're discussing, it's psychiatry.'

The sergeant took it with an ill grace. Stubbornly, he said: 'But there's concrete evidence against him as well.

The time of night he left the Fraser Arms, the buttons we picked up on the Whinny Knowe . . .'

'A lot of people were out and about in Kilcolum between eight and eight-thirty last night. The buttons belonged to his waterproof all right, but the various strands of material we found caught in the girl's fingernails and on the whin bush near the body were none of them from Fraser's suit, which is of light grey worsted. Nor were they from Mary Allen's clothes . . .'

There was a sober knock at the door.

Constable Reid came in, an air of surprise making his ruddy face appear even more youthfully anxious than usual. 'Miss Thomson would like a word with you, sir. She's on her way to the service in the kirk.'

'Miss Thomson? Oh, yes, the minister's sister. Show her in.'

Kate refused Greenlees's invitation to sit down. She wore a dark grey suit and a small black hat with a fringe of black veiling.

She said: 'Something has occurred to me, in connection with Mary Allen's death. According to Constable Reid, it may be news to you.'

She was pale but controlled. The inspector, a comfortably married man, thought she looked charming, as a minister's sister ought to look. MacKinlay, who was a bachelor, thought she had a smashing figure and gorgeous hair but detected in her general attitude an ability to keep smart operators at a distance. He had experience in this line of country.

'Yes, Miss Thomson?' Greenlees was encouraging.

'I—I saw the body when it was brought in from the golf course. I'm almost certain there was no bracelet on her arm. Can you confirm this?'

He riffled through the medical reports. 'The girl wore

no jewellery,' he said, finally. 'Indeed, I can vouch for that myself from personal knowledge.'

He was standing over her, like a bulky shadow. She fiddled with her gloves. 'Mrs Allen told me this morning that Mary was wearing a bracelet when she went off to the Brownie meeting.'

'I see.' He gestured to MacKinlay to take notes. 'What kind of bracelet?'

'Grace Allen didn't say. As far as I can remember, her exact words were—"I let her wear the bracelet last night. She found it in a drawer and always wanted it." '

'That was all?'

'Yes.'

Hunched over the table, MacKinlay said: 'Strange that neither Mr nor Mrs Allen mentioned this. They saw the body, too.'

She glanced down at him. 'I don't suppose they were in a condition to notice details.' Her voice was cool.

Greenlees nodded. 'That probably accounts for it.' After a moment he said: 'What about yourself, Miss Thomson? You were in charge of the Brownies in the Hall last night. Did you happen to see the bracelet?'

She shook her head. 'I've been trying to think back, but we were all so busy I simply didn't notice.'

'H'm. Understandable, in the circumstances. Well, thank you, Miss Thomson. If there's nothing else . . .'

'Nothing. I'm going to the church. Are you?'

'Yes.'

Slipping the notes he had made into a folder, MacKinlay rose and said: 'One of the best times to catch people off their guard is at a funeral service.'

Greenlees ignored him. He took his cap, gloves and

cane from the top of the bookcase. 'May I walk with you to the church?' he said to Kate.

'Of course,' she answered.

The Rev. Harry Thomson was pacing up and down the softly lit vestry, mentally rehearsing the short address he planned to give during the service. A table covered with red baize stood near an electric fire. On it were neatly arranged his white linen bands, his order of servide, his praise-list.

Willie the Bomber came in, clad in the beadle's traditional dark blue suit. His moustache seemed to be more luxurious, more rustily red than usual. This was of the amount of oil he had spread on it to keep it in place.

'Twenty past six, sir.' His voice was pitched down to an uncharacteristic unction. 'Robing time, eh?'

'Yes.'

Harry Thomson took off his black jacket. Willie tied twin bands about his collar, fragile emblems of ordination. Then, removing a glossy black gown from a hanger behind the door, he held it high while the minister shrugged himself into its voluminous folds. Finally, across the shoulders of the gown he carefully arranged the hood, trimmed with maroon silk, which indicated that its wearer was an Arts graduate of Glasgow University.

He stood back and surveyed the result. 'A wee bit o' fluff on the skirt o' the gown, sir. Wait you a minute.'

He took a clothes-brush from a drawer in the table.

When he had finished, he sighed and said: 'That's you ready, sir. But I can see you're no' in your usual good trim.'

94

'I've never had to do anything like this before. I feel terrible.'

'Ay, it's no' easy. But you'll manage, sir. I know fine you'll manage, once you get started.'

'Is there a big congregation?'

'There's folk in there tonight that haven't been at an ordinary service in a month o' Sundays!'

'What comfort can I give them? I feel so inadequate, Willie. How can I explain to the Allens that the death of their daughter is God's will?'

'You'll do it, sir. Just say what's in your heart.'

'There's anger in my heart. That's the trouble. I keep remembering that in a few minutes I may be preaching to a murderer.'

'If the murderer is the kind o' man we suspect he is, maybe he'll need more sympathy than anybody.'

'There's that, of course.'

Willie saw a flash of pain and self-loathing in the minister's eyes. He felt suddenly uneasy, uncomfortable. He fumbled in his waistcoat pocket and consulted the big silver watch he'd inherited from his father. 'Twenty-five past, sir. I'd better go and ring the bell.'

'Sure. Say a prayer for everybody concerned while you're at it.'

'I'll try, sir.'

When he had gone, the minister resumed his pacing. He had made only a few turns, however, when the door opened.

From the passage outside Kate said: 'Excuse me, Harry. Inspector Greenlees would like a word with you. It's important.'

'Of course.'

She guided him in, then went off to join the choir assembling in the session-house.

The big policeman closed the door behind him. 'Forgive the intrusion, Mr Thomson, especially at a time like this. I was wondering if you'd care to co-operate by making two intimations tonight.'

'On behalf of the police?'

'Yes. First, a warning to parents. Children going out during the day should always be accompanied by an adult. After dark they should be kept indoors.'

'I'll do that, Inspector.' He scribbled a note on the back of his praise-list. 'It comes very much within the scope of the Church's duty.'

'Thank you, sir.'

'And the second intimation?'

'An appeal to anyone who happened to be in the vicinity of Riverside Street between eight and half-past eight last night to get in touch with us.'

Harry Thomson made another note. 'Very good, Inspector.'

The bell in the short blunt steeple began to ring. It sounded dull, out of tune like the people of Kilcolum. Late-comers who had been talking on the pavement outside began to move into the church past the lighted vestry window.

He looked up at Greenlees, trying not to flinch as he said: 'So you believe there's a maniac at work?'

'We're bound to take precautions, sir.'

'Does that mean you're not absolutely certain?'

'Personally, I'm by no means certain. In fact, the picture of a sex maniac on the prowl is unlikely in my opinion.'

'A sheep was strangled, then Mary Allen . . .'

'I have my doubts about that sheep. We've spoken to the vet and to Mr Craig. The vet admits he had drink taken the afternoon he examined her. He now says the

96

mark on her throat might have been caused by the clinging branch of a bramble-bush. Archie Craig tells us that
a ewe in lamb chokes very easily. If she got entangled in
a bush she could panic and in a few minutes virtually
strangle herself. There's another point. Not conclusive
but at any rate suggestive. Mary Allen wasn't sexually
assaulted.'

The minister nodded. 'You told that to the Allens.
It was a relief to them.' He put a hand on the other's
arm. 'Let's hope to God you're right about the ewe,
Inspector.'

The bell stopped.

Greenlees said: 'I'll be getting inside, then. I'm grateful for your co-operation.'

As he left, Willie came bustling in. 'The choir's lined
up, sir. I'll lead them in if you're ready.'

'I'm ready,' said Harry Thomson.

He picked up his order of service and praise-list. His
knuckles were white.

The interior of the church was a mixture of ancient
and modern.

The whitewashed walls, buttressed by baulks of tim-
ber stained dark brown; the gallery supported by
wooden pillars of the same colour; the raftered roof
with the bell-rope disappearing into a cavity below the
steeple—all this had scarcely changed in two hundred
years.

But in the deep, embrasured windows there was a
glowing collection of stained glass, most of it presented
to the church in recent years by various individuals and
organisations wishing to commemorate dead relatives
and friends. The pews, of a comfortable modern style,
glinted in the light from ornate electric chandeliers. The

97

main aisle and the side passages were covered by thick red carpeting.

Standing under the high pulpit and flanked by artistically carved choir stalls, the organ was new, electrically powered. John Knox would have declaimed against its use in public worship. So, in fact, had old Isaac Semple. But two years ago, more liberal spirits in the congregation like Peter Fraser, Jimmy Young and Dan Sillars had voted for what they called progress but what old Isaac called idolatry.

Tonight almost every pew was filled with people. Steam heat was wafted up through grid-lanes in the stone floor. There was a faint pervading odour of damp bibles.

Alec sat at the outer end of the laird's pew, which was situated below the pulpit, facing it and the choir. Peter and Meg were beside him, on his left. They were holding hands. Sometimes they whispered together, heads close.

He felt exposed and vulnerable in the centre of the church. Eyes watched him from the gallery above and from either side in the area.

He knew how the minds of the Kilcolum folk were working. He had gone away to seek his fortune, turning his back on his native parish. They had heard about Elizabeth. They were unwilling to face the fact that one of their number might be a murderer. He represented, therefore, a convenient scapegoat.

It was a cruel way of reasoning but a human one. He didn't blame them for the thoughts behind their eyes. They were basically kind and hospitable, and in a sense their attitude was impersonal. It was his bad luck that he had stumbled into such a situation. In other circumstances they would soon have overcome their shyness of him as a comparative stranger and welcomed him home again as one of themselves.

A grey-haired teacher with a fur stole and a black straw hat was playing gentle Hebridean airs on the organ. She was Miss Agnes Rutherford, a colleague of Jenny's on the staff of the infant school. In spite of his feeling of isolation, Alec was conscious of comparative peace, something he had missed during recent months. He found that in this new atmosphere of calm his mental processes were becoming clearer and more logical.

Thinking of the service caused him to dwell for a time on the reason for it, the pathetic little body of Mary Allen.

It had first been examined by the police and the doctors, then taken home for identification by her father and mother. Now it lay in the mortuary of the Cottage Hospital in Stewarton. Tomorrow a pathologist would arrive from the Forensic Medicine Department of Glasgow University to carry out a complete post mortem on behalf of the Procurator Fiscal. But from what had been said by the police surgeon and Jimmy Young, it was almost a foregone conclusion that the final verdict would be death by strangulation. A charge of murder would soon be preferred against somebody.

Against whom?

Alec's thoughts were filled with compassion for the Allens and with hatred of the person who had killed their daughter. He was no longer so afraid that he himself might be to blame.

His talk with Kate had brought about a partial return of common sense and confidence. His mind had been a cupboard stuffed with old junk and fungus. She had cleaned it out with ruthless efficiency, leaving it clean and bright and open to the air. Now he could contemplate his own actions with some objectivity—his impulse to confess that he'd strangled Elizabeth, his fear of the Ardcapple bridge, his flight to the Whinny Knowe.

Kate had been right. In the case of Elizabeth, he had been the victim of a guilt complex. He had *felt* like strangling Elizabeth, and his tortured, drug-sodden mind had confused temptation with reality. In the case of the bridge, he had shied away from it because of Peter's story about Nancy MacKay and his own unreasoning fear that he might glimpse her dead body in the river. As for his flight to the Whinny Knowe, this had been an instinctive reaction based on boyish memories of hiding there from his father.

He sighed, glad that he had recovered the power of logical analysis, sad that so many people in Kilcolum should be inclined to suspect him of the murder of a little girl.

Was the murderer here in church? Slowly he looked about him, noticing as he did so that some eyes were lowered and expressions frozen.

He saw Jimmy Young and his dark-haired wife in the front pew of the gallery. In her thin, intelligent face was subdued sadness. In his the hearty ruddiness had faded. He looked weary, drawn and grey. Beside them were the Heathergills, the Commander's bushy white hair in startling contrast with the brick-red of his clean-shaven cheeks. Mrs Heathergill was angular and prim, with a black hat functionally plain. Her aquiline features expressed an aristocratic acceptance of tragedy.

In the area he picked out other faces.

Willie the Bomber's mother wore a drab black coat and a black scarf on her straggly white hair. Her wrinkled face was softened by a kind of monumental patience with life. Archie Craig and his wife looked uneasy and unhappy in this atmosphere of suffering. Mrs Craig caught Alec's eye and nodded and smiled a little.

Two pews in the east area were filled with the older children from the school. Next to the aisle in one of them was the senior infant teacher, Mrs Grant, usually serene and comfortable but tonight formal in a slightly outmoded suit of dark grey. Next to the aisle in the other was Dan Sillars. He looked worried and somehow dishevelled. When two boys exchanged whispers he turned his head and silenced them with a scowl.

The Semple pew in the east area held four people.

Beside old Isaac, who sat grim and erect with folded arms, Alec saw Tom Allen, his thin face pasty with sorrow. Grace Allen wasn't there. She was at home with Mrs MacKay, unable in her agony to face a congregation of her neighbours.

Along the seat, near the wall, were young Isaac and his wife. Isaac and his grandfather, though separated by only four feet of space, seemed unaware of each other. Mourning hadn't brought them together any more than happiness. And that young Isaac and his Virginia were happy together was evident in the way they sat, quiet and close, their shoulders touching.

Incongruously, it occurred to Alec to wonder who might be looking after the cocktail bar in the Fraser Arms. The manager himself, he guessed.

In the pew at the main door he spotted Sergeant MacKinlay. As they exchanged glances, wary but unemotional, Greenlees came in and sat down beside his colleague. His uniform and solid presence caused a stir in the church like the sound of wind in a barley-field.

Double doors were opened with authority. Footsteps came smartly down the aisle as Willie led in the choir. He stood stiff and solemn in one of the side-passages until about a dozen people, including Kate and Jenny, had filed past him into the carved stalls, until the minister, robes fluttering, had mounted the short flight of steps to the pulpit. Then he went back and closed the double doors.

As the organist reached the end of her voluntary, he came and sat beside Alec. He smiled and patted his shoulder.

In the face of the congregation Willie was showing his allegiance. It was such a brave and unexpected gesture that a lump of gratitude came into Alec's throat.

9

THE service was short and simple. Harry Thomson looked years older than he was. His brief sermon sounded almost apologetic until near the end he touched the fringe of a mystery.

'The bereaved parents, the relatives and friends of this little girl, they must question in their hearts the efficacy of prayer. What is the explanation of prayer? I remember tonight something my mother said when my father died. "I asked God to cure him," she said. "I prayed day and night. But it seems that though we are encouraged to pray for help, we must always remember that God sometimes says no." '

Alec listened and rediscovered remnants of a long-neglected faith. He glanced towards the choir stalls.

Jenny was sitting straight-backed and still, her face expressionless. She moved a little, as if aware of his scrutiny. Tears glinted on her cheeks. He felt tenderness and sympathy. He was suddenly convinced that for some reason unconnected with the tragedy she was unhappy and under strain. He wanted to comfort her. He wanted to hear about her unhappiness so that he could try to conjure it away. He wanted to see her smile as she had smiled at him so long ago, impulsively, with no hint of wariness. He realised that on their two recent meetings he had scarcely once seen her smile.

He looked along the stall. Kate's head turned quickly and he knew she had been watching him. Her face, too, was expressionless. Her whole attention appeared to be concentrated on her brother in the pulpit. But he saw a flicker of something in her eyes which might have been pain. Or even anger.

The sermon finished. The final psalm was sung. Miss Rutherford began to play, and the congregation rose. The tune on the organ was vaguely familiar. He came out of the church under the street lights, with people jostling round him in sad silence, and remembered what it was: *Hebridean Cradle Song.*

Waiting for Peter and Meg, he nodded to the Youngs and the Heathergills. Jimmy Young approached, caught his arm and said: 'See you later, I hope.' Alec wondered what he meant.

With her husband looming behind her, Mrs Craig bobbed out of the crowd. She shook hands with Alec, as determined as Willie to demonstrate friendliness and trust. 'Come and see us again,' she said, in a clear, carrying voice. 'Come soon, Alec.'

Impulsively he bent down and kissed her cheek, with its thin scent of powder.

Archie Craig put a hand on his shoulder. 'That goes for all of us,' he said.

Tom Allen shuffled past, head bowed, a long, un-fashionable coat flapping open round his calves. He was going back to weeping women, with rest and sleep a hope only for the future.

The children had been marshalled on the pavement, Dan Sillars and Mrs Grant fussing round them like warders as their parents arrived to claim them. Now Dan's duties were over. He saw Alec and came and spoke to him, face lined and grey.

'Thank God that's over! I hate it when they make an orgy of a funeral. When we're dead we're dead. I want my body to be burnt and my ashes scattered on the river, and to hell with weeping and wailing! Funerals!' he said, between clenched teeth.

'They indicate respect. Not only for the dead. For the relatives ...'

'If people would show you that kind of respect when you're alive I could understand it. But do they? Not bloody likely!' He stopped, took a quick breath, put a lanky arm about Alec. 'Sorry, son. I'm being crude, as usual. See you at the Big House.'

He moved away to look for Jenny.

A voice behind Alec said, harshly: 'It surprises me to see *you* in church!'

He turned. Old Isaac Semple was buttoning a long black overcoat about his neck.

'Why should you be surprised, Mr Semple?'

The craggy face was stern; the deep-set eyes were cold as ice. 'We've heard about your life in London. A city of sin, a Sodom and Gomorrah. You should have stayed there.'

Alec was at first too astonished to be angry. That anybody with such an outlook could exist in the second half of the twentieth century was a shock to him. Here

104

was the voice of obsessional puritanism, a voice he imagined had become silent a hundred years ago.

He said: 'I came to church to mourn the death of a little girl. Surely even a sinner can do that?'

'You were drunk last night. A disgrace to Kilcolum and to your father's name.' The words were loud. In groups lingering on the street heads were turned. 'Did you think of mourning a little girl last night?'

Now anger came shuddering in. 'What do you mean by that?'

'Take what meaning you like. This is a quiet, douce parish. Evildoers poison it, like germs in fresh meat.'

Alec sighed. The situation was becoming droll, even grotesque.

He said: 'So you set yourself up as a judge of good and evil?'

'I believe in the Lord. He guides me to do His will I seek out evil and destroy it.'

'Good for you! One of the Lord's elect, eh?'

'I do His will.'

'Then why don't you try seeking out good for a change?'

The bony face with its sprout of grey bristle was suddenly twisted. Eavesdroppers began to walk away, embarrassed. Alec caught sight of Peter and Meg going towards the car parked by the kerb. It was his car, the pale green Cortina. He turned away, too, and began to move after them, tired of the argument and saddened by the grim enmity of this elder of the Kirk. But old Isaac shot out a scrawny left arm and gripped his shoulder.

'You're clever, Alec Fraser. You have the gift of words. But tell me this, what was your car doing on the golf course road last night?'

105

'My car?'

'We're simple folk here in Kilcolum. You think you can fool us, but . . .'

'Let him go, Grandfather!'

Alec swung round. The steel-strong fingers loosed their hold on his waterproof. The hand was lifted clear.

'That's better,' said young Isaac. His wife's hand was on his arm.

'What business is it of yours?' The old man's voice, though still harsh, was now less confident.

'The good name of the Semple family is my business. You know that, Grandfather.' And when there was no answer, young Isaac continued: 'Kilcolum has a reputation for hospitality. I should hate it if Mr Fraser got the wrong impression from you.'

Old Isaac stared at his grandson. Hate was gradually controlled and hidden behind a blank expression. Then he hunched a shoulder and walked away, long legs splaying as if he found it difficult to maintain a balance.

'I'm sorry,' said young Isaac, shaking his head. 'But I expect you know my grandfather, the kind of man he is. Sometimes he imagines he is Abraham and Isaac and Jacob rolled into one. People here make allowances.' His momentary anger had drained away, giving place to warmth. He went on, quickly: 'My wife, Virginia. Mr. Alec Fraser.'

They shook hands. Her clasp was firm, her blue eyes frank. She was probably about twenty-seven, he thought, slimly built, unremarkable in looks. Her hair was straight, an indeterminate light brown. Yet he sensed in her an unruffled will, a calm ability to face and control unpleasant circumstances. He guessed it was from Virginia that young Isaac had drawn courage to face his

106

accusers in the parish and to embark on the rough tides of journalism.

'We're on our way home,' she said. 'Isaac has the night off. Won't you come and have a drink with us?'

He remembered that Dan and Jenny were coming to the Big House later in the evening and was about to explain this when young Isaac said: 'Please, Mr Fraser. Even if it's only for a few minutes.'

He was suddenly eager to accept the invitation. The prospect of talking shop with a fellow writer—even an apprentice writer—was attractive. He liked young Isaac and his wife. Their approach was fresh, straightforward, unsuspicious. And as he now admitted to himself he needed a diversion like this to take his mind off an imminent social duty for which he had little stomach.

He said: 'Thanks. I'd like that very much. Give me a second to tell Peter and Meg.'

As he helped her into the car, Meg said: 'All right, Alec. Dinner's at eight. Dad and Jenny will be arriving about half-past.'

'I've just seen the minister and his sister,' Peter explained. 'They're coming round, too. Also the doctor and his wife if Jimmy has no urgent calls. Meg and I thought it might do us all good to have a quiet get-together. It's been such a hell of a day.' He looked up from the wheel. 'Anyway,' he pointed out, 'you're a bit of an attraction. The prodigal son, that kind of thing.' With some anxiety, he added: 'You'll walk back from the cottage?'

'Yes. It won't take me ten minutes.'

'Good. Don't—don't let us down.'

Alec knew he had been about to add 'again' but had cut himself short. 'I won't let you down,' he promised.

107

He watched his own Cortina move off, three problems yeasting in his mind.

What lay behind old Isaac Semple's reference to his car?

How was he going to face Jenny and appear at ease, now that Kate Thomson would be present as well as Dan?

And what was making Peter so cagey, so unnaturally withdrawn, so shifty even?

As he went to rejoin the young Semples, he realised that in the porch of the church, standing in the grey shadows, Inspector Greenlees had been listening to everything that had been said.

The small living-room of the cottage was furnished with pieces which were mainly second-hand but had a certain distinction. On the cream distempered walls were three original paintings, one of Virginia as a teenager, another of Kilcolum from Columba's Crag, the third of the Breckrie, with the sea in the distance. Alec guessed that this last artist had placed his easel on or near the Ardcapple bridge.

Taking bottles and glasses from the solid oak sideboard, young Isaac said: 'Virginia's uncle painted her on the day she was told she'd passed five A-level exams. That accounts for the smug look on her face!'

'She looks beautiful,' said Alec. 'Nearly as beautiful as she does now.'

Virginia laughed. 'Why don't you ever say nice things like that, Isaac?'

She drew the curtains and sat down in one of the two armchairs by the fire, motioning Alec into the other.

At the sideboard, Isaac smiled and said: 'Whisky, Mr Fraser?'

'A very small one, please, with plenty of soda. As you know, I had an experience with whisky last night.'

Hastily, Isaac went on: 'The other two pictures I got from an artist who stayed in the hotel last year. Quite a character. About seventy or eighty he was, a retired railwayman, tough as nails. He'd wanted to paint all his life and was now able to indulge his fancy, thanks in part to a win on the pools. The pictures were a kind of tip. I'd looked after him so well in the bar, he said.'

Alec nodded. 'I'm not an expert, but they look first-class.'

'When we're rich,' Virginia told him, 'we'll make these the basis of our big collection.'

Isaac gave his wife a glass of sherry, then filled up Alec's tumbler with soda water. He took his own whisky. Thin and awkward-looking, he sat on a straight-backed chair between his wife and his guest.

He said: 'Do journalists ever get rich, Mr Fraser? Freelances, I mean?'

'Some do. It's a matter of luck, I think. If you're really serious, my advice would be to try writing a book. Fact or fiction. Get your name before the public. Then have a go at radio and television. Papers and magazines are more difficult. Nowadays most of them get their copy from people on the staff or commission it from big names.'

'I told you, darling.' Virginia was obviously as keen on shop as her husband. 'In fact, Mr Fraser, Isaac has an idea for a book right now. A Burgess and MacLean spy story. He was never a party member, of course, but he came in contact with several communists in Glasgow and has a fair knowledge of how they think and act.'

Isaac put in: 'I visited Moscow once, with a party of

students, and should be strong enough on local Russian colour. I took plenty of notes.'

'When I was a secretary I went to Germany many times. With my boss. Mostly to the Leipzig Trade Fair.' Virginia was enthusiastic. 'I could supply background in that direction.'

Alec was surprised and impressed. Here was a young couple who in other circumstances might have been among the so-called 'international set'. Lack of money and opportunity kept them in Kilcolum; but their outlook was neither restricted nor parochial. In fact, he thought, aware of a bookcase crammed with books, papers and magazines and of a radio and television set in a corner, their view of the world and its behaviour was perhaps in clearer perspective than that of some who lived and worked at the sources of news and whose picture of events was therefore blurred by proximity.

He said: 'I think you should go ahead on this. I might be able to help by introducing you to a good agent. And if the book does happen to be accepted, I know the literary editor on the *Messenger* and could perhaps suggest a review.'

The pleasure and excitement in their eyes caused him a pang of guilt. 'Mind you,' he said, quickly, 'all this is a matter of ifs and buts. And in the end, even if the book *is* published, even if it does get a good review, it may sell only a few hundred copies.'

They nodded wisely, but he perceived that the economics of the case didn't worry them. Isaac was born to be a writer. With Virginia's co-operation he would continue to write, come hell or high-water, and his very persistence might lift him to success.

The talk continued for half an hour. It seemed shorter to Alec. The young Semples quizzed him about life in

Fleet Street. He made polite inquires about them.

He knew that Isaac's father and mother had died of influenza when he was a baby; that he'd been brought up by his grandmother, old Isaac's wife. What he learnt now was that after his grandmother's death, when he was about fourteen, his relationship with old Isaac had, over the years, gradually gone from bad to worse. His reference to their final break was curt and somehow unconvincing. Alec suspected that this might be due less to natural reticence about a private quarrel than to some dark and hurtful memory.

Virginia, it turned out, had experienced no comparable family drama. Her father worked for a building firm as a master mason and lived quietly with her mother, a stalwart of the Woman's Guild, in East Kilbride near Glasgow. Undoubtedly, this background was the source of her stable character. Alec wished all writers—in fact, all artists exposed to the shattering disappointments and triumphs of their calling—could be supplied with wives of a similar calibre.

At twenty to eight he finally said good night, amidst a chatter of mutual esteem. He reached the Big House at ten to eight and heard Meg calling from the kitchen: 'Well done, Alec! Dead on time. Peter has a drink for you in the library.'

Hanging his waterproof on the hallstand, he heard a metallic chink coming from the left-hand outside pocket. He groped inside and drew out a silver chain bracelet. It was unfastened, and the slender catch had been broken. Attached to the links was a round, shallow receptacle like a locket, which, though now empty, might once have contained a miniature painting or a photograph. Its lid sagged open.

111

10

As far as Alec was concerned, the evening was a continual strain. He mentioned the bracelet to nobody. It lay in his trousers pocket, its hardness continually perceptible through the lining. It gave him no peace, a burr against his flesh like the burr against his spirit represented by the presence of both Jenny and Kate.

The Youngs had been able to come after all. Lucy Young was mini-skirted and slim, though her lean face seemed old in comparison with her dress and figure. She had been a nurse, and some of the nurse's clinical assurance was still evident after ten years of marriage. She and Meg chattered and did their best to avoid the subject of Mary Allen's death.

Up to a point they were successful, and as the evening went on, and Peter's slightly overpitched hospitality showed no sign of flagging, the party became almost gay. For a time Harry Thomson found relief from his burden of inadequacy in the face of sorrow. For a time Dan Sillars put the thought of evil aside and amused his listeners with stories about some long-forgotten characters who had lived in Kilcolum. Jimmy Young's loud laughter became more frequent as he countered Dan's stories with medical reminiscences of his own.

Jenny drank gin diluted with tonic water. She smiled at Dan's jokes. But always, as she smiled, her eyes turned towards Alec. Her face was a little flushed. She sat on the arm of a chair, her short cocktail frock revealing slender thighs. She was more desirable to him now than she had ever been. He remembered her in his arms and a

112

sense of frustration and loss made his temples beat. But he tried to talk and act with normal courtesy and for a while was able to discipline the uneasiness building up inside him.

Kate Thomson drank only lemonade. She sat on a stool by his feet, her red head almost touching his knees. She hadn't changed her dark grey suit. Unlike Jenny, she seemed austere, almost aloof. But he remembered their meeting that afternoon under Columba's Crag. He remembered her diagnosis of his trouble, her ability to analyse and dismiss his fears. He remembered the hint she had given him of a secret guilt of her own. He remembered her crying.

At one point the superficial gaiety skirted the edge of reality. Harry Thomson said something about Mary Allen's mother. 'Wasn't she Grace MacKay before she married?' he asked.

'Right,' Dan said. 'A cousin of the Nancy MacKay who fell from the bridge. About ten years older, of course, but out of the same drawer. Man daft, I'd say. But Tom Allen took charge of her, encouraged by his boss, old Isaac, who is said to have arranged the match as a Christian duty. Tom was an ageing bachelor, turning to drink for company. Grace was running after men. They were good for each other. And indeed their child Mary was a splendid lassie, with the good points of both her parents and only a few of their bad ones.'

Jimmy Young said: 'There's a rumour going round that the murderer took a bracelet she was wearing. One that belonged to her mother.'

'It's no rumour,' Kate told him, and the lack of surprise in the general reaction made it apparent that her knowledge was shared. 'Though of course,' she added, 'there's no evidence that the murderer took it. All that

113

can be said, according to Inspector Greenlees, is that Mary had it on her arm when she left the house and hadn't when they found her.'

Dan turned to the doctor. 'In that case,' he said, 'your theory about a maniac may be a bit screwy!'

The other shook his head, looking worried and uncertain. 'Depends on what you mean by maniac. You have the murderer who kills because he can't resist his own distorted sexual impulses. This is the generally accepted definition of a maniac. But you also have the murderer who kills systematically for gain, material or social, and to my way of thinking you can't differentiate between the two. You can't describe the one as "insane and therefore irresponsible" and the other as "sane but wicked". The man or woman who quietly but determinedly kills for personal gain is as far removed from the normalities of social behaviour as your more flamboyant Kürtens and Jack the Rippers.'

'Then,' said Dan, with a snarl of sarcasm, 'you'd claim all murderers are maniacs?'

'Generalisations are always difficult. But wouldn't you agree that if somebody kills to—to satisfy his lust, for example, then goes on killing to cover up his tracks, wouldn't you agree that such a person is abnormal, devoid of ordinary human feeling? In other words, a maniac?'

'Like Christie of Rillington Place?'

'Yes. Christie is as good an example of the quiet, systematic murderer as one could find.'

Dan nodded. 'Well, you may be right, Jimmy. Anyway, it's an interesting theory.'

In some distress Harry Thomson put in: 'But surely we're not dealing with a Christie in Kilcolum. May not

114

Mary Allen's murder be a kind of accident—an isolated accident?'

'If it were,' said Dan, 'I'm pretty sure that by this time the killer would have broken down and confessed. According to Jimmy—and for once I agree with him—this would be the normal reaction.'

Alec felt sick. The watered whisky in his glass tasted raw. His stomach turned against it. A migraine was threatening. What he said now was triggered off by tension, and he was as much surprised by his own vehemence as were the others.

'There's something evil in Kilcolum. I've been conscious of it ever since I came back. I think Mary Allen may have died because by chance she discovered its source.'

Jenny's eyes were suddenly big with anxiety. No longer did she try to camouflage her concern. He saw in her face a deep personal involvement in his mood and realised that her coolness towards him had been a kind of camouflage. Momentarily his words had stripped a corner bare.

Lucy Young said, brightly: 'Oh, for goodness' sake, we're getting morbid! It's your fault, Jimmy.'

'Always is, my pet.'

'You should write a paper about murder for the *Lancet* and get all those theories out of your system.' She shook her head, canvassing for sympathy with thin, ringed hands. 'He's terrible, you know. If it's not golf, it's murder. He keeps a pile of books by his bedside—ghastly things! Paperbacks mostly: *The Meaning of Murder, Unfit to Plead?, The Woman in the Case, True Murder Mysteries*. It's an obsession with him.'

Her husband laughed. 'She goes to bed with *Dr*

Kildare's Secret or *Nurses in Love* or something awful like that. My murders are in self-defence.'

Most of the others laughed, too, more loudly than they might have done had the desire for relief and change of subject not been so insistent. But Jenny was still watching Alec, and Dan, old and grey and more unkempt than usual, had become aware of her interest in him.

At Alec's feet Kate was fiddling with her glass. She had seen the look in Jenny's eyes. She wanted to turn round in order to discover the quality of response in his, but the effort was beyond her.

Meg began to talk about Peter's taste in reading. 'He's an old square, let me tell you. Give him something historical or antiquarian and I might as well not exist until he's finished reading it. Can you imagine, one day on our honeymoon in the Hebrides he took me to see an ugly great stone circle, and instead of being romantic—as I expected him to be—he lectured me about it all afternoon! Druidical, he said. Very significant. Though significant of what I still don't know!'

Peter had been drinking more than usual, and his reply came uncharacteristically hearty and loud. 'She's a young Philistine. I can never make her understand that you always build for the future on the foundation of the past.'

She came and sat on his knee, putting one arm about his neck and waving her tumbler of lemonade with the other. 'But I do understand, darling. That's why you must now forget about Druids and start reading books on baby-care.' She appealed to everyone. 'Can you imagine him pinning on nappies? I think his education was dreadfully neglected.'

Peter didn't join in the laughter. Impulsively, he drew

116

his wife close, resting his head against her. She was surprised and even a little alarmed.

'What is it?' she said.

He released her. 'Nothing. Let's have another drink.'

At half-past ten Meg said: 'But you musn't go yet. Wait until you've had a cup of tea. Come on, Jenny. Help me brew up in the kitchen.'

They had been gone for only a few minutes when Alec excused himself. His headache was getting worse. All day he had avoided pills. Now he felt an urgent need of them to soothe away the pain.

The box was in his bedroom upstairs. He swallowed two with a mouthful of water from the tap in the washhand basin, then switched off the light and returned along the corridor.

He heard quick footsteps mounting the stairs. He paused in the shadows on the landing just as Jenny came into sight.

She reached the top and saw him. She paused, too, and they stood there, only a few feet apart, trying to recover poise like runners after a race.

She stepped into the shadows. She said: 'Alec, you're being terribly hurt. I can't bear you being hurt.'

She was looking up at him, her lips parted, her breath uneven. The years rolled back. They were alone in the moonlight at the back of the new Hall. Music for the dance was swinging inside. His throat was dry.

He bent his head against her cheek and whispered: 'Jenny, I need you.'

'I know, Alec. I know.' Her hand was behind his head, stroking it.

'But I thought ...'

Her hand came round and touched his face. She was

117

crying. 'Dan is good and kind. He needs me, too. I thought you had forgotten me.'

'Maybe I had. But ever since I met you again, yesterday, I've been remembering. That night in the barley . . .'

'Oh, Alec.'

'I want you, Jenny.'

Her body fitted against his, lithe and warm and eager as he remembered it. There was a scent among the tumble of her hair that he remembered, too. He kissed her mouth, her cheek, her neck. Desire grew between them as it had done so long ago, flaring as they stumbled a little against the corridor wall.

She sobbed and strained away. She said: 'I can't believe it. This shouldn't have happened.'

He drew her back to him. Her resistance crumbled again. Her arms went round him, and she hid her face against his chest. 'I love you, Alec. I've always loved you. I told myself it couldn't be.'

'I'm not fit to touch you,' he said, headache forgotten.

'Hold me, darling. Hold me close!'

There was a quick flurry of low heels on the polished floor of the hall downstairs. 'Jenny, where are you?'

He released her and she stood aside, panting. With an effort of will which carved out lines at each corner of her mouth, she regained control. 'Coming, Meg,' she called.

'Haven't you finished powdering your nose yet? The tea's infused.'

'I'm sorry. I got lost in all those corridors.'

The door of the drawing-room opened, driving a swathe of yellow light across the dimness of the hall. Kate Thomson stood silhouetted against the glow.

She glanced upstairs, her body stiff, her whole attitude revealing unhappiness.

She said: 'Meg, can I help you?'

'It's all right, Kate. Jenny's just coming.'

Jenny went down, leaving Alec alone.

The party ended at about half-past eleven. The cars crunched away from the front door steps, the minister and his sister in the first, Lucy and Jimmy Young in the second, Dan and Jenny in the third.

The minister, the doctor and the schoolmaster: each, thought Alec, with a powerful influence in the parish either for good or evil. In these democratic days not even the laird could wield a greater authority.

Their comparative financial standing was exemplified in their cars. The minister's pale blue Hillman Imp was noisy, a little rusty under the doors, in need of a respray. The doctor's cream Volkswagen, though mud-stained after a day on country side-tracks, was new and powerful, the engine efficiently tuned. The schoolmaster's off-white Austin was clean and in good condition, but Dan had bought it years ago, and in consequence it looked old-fashioned.

Alec's headache had gone, but he was tired. His logic was awry. He'd held Jenny in his arms and kissed her. He'd listened to her admission that she loved him. But the thrill of it all was passing, and he felt guilty in regard to Kate and Dan.

Kate had offered him frank and uninhibited friendship. She had understood his need for confession and had helped skilfully to rid his mind of an ugly fantasy. Jenny had been on her guard, careful to maintain an attitude proper in a girl engaged to another man. And yet it was Jenny who with one word of sympathy had made him act like a boy again in his need for affection.

But what of Kate, to whom he owed so much, her eyes

119

hurt and almost angry as she tried to exchange tea-cup banalities with him in the drawing-room? And what of Dan, the fire gone out him, burdened by the weight of his age as he gruffly suggested to Jenny it was time to go?

He tried to analyse his feelings but was too confused to reach a conclusion. The events of the past thirty-six hours had come crowding in too fast. The death of a little girl had upset his confidence and sense of balance. Now danger lurked in the shadows, symbolised by a bracelet in his pocket, making him uncertain even of his own motives and reactions.

When everybody had gone, Peter persuaded Meg to forget the party cups and glasses. He and Alec, he said, would wash up and lay the table for breakfast.

'Angel!' she said, touching his hand. 'I'll get off to bed, then. Please don't be too long. Good night, Alec. Sleep well.'

In the kitchen the brothers tackled their chores in silence, each busy with his own thoughts.

At one point Peter said: 'What possessed Jenny Craig to say she'd marry Dan? Have you worked it out? When they marry she'll be my mother-in-law! And I'm ten years older.'

Alec was polishing the slim-stemmed glass from which Jenny had drunk her gin. His back was towards Peter. Slowly and stiffly, without turning, he said: 'It's Jenny's own business.'

'Sure. I'm not criticising her. But she's so douce and quiet compared with Dan. So vulnerable, in a way.' He glanced at his brother. Arranging dishes and cutlery on a tray, he went on: 'Well, if you're ready I'll take this lot through to the dining-room and lay the table. You take the glasses and park them in the sideboard.'

'Right.'

Afterwards they went across to the empty, smoke-stale drawing-room, where the embers of a peat fire still glowed in the hearth.

Lack of colour in Peter's stout cheeks made him look tired, in need of a shave. 'A final cigarette?' He offered his case.

Alec took one, made a spill of paper and lit it from the fire. He straightened up. 'You heard what Kate Thomson said about the bracelet?'

'Yes. Important, d'you think?'

'It's important to me, Peter. I found this in the pocket of my waterproof about four hours ago.'

He held it out on the palm of his hand. Silver links sparkled in the light.

Horror showed in Peter's face. 'Is this—is this the bracelet they're talking about?'

'I reckon it's an odds-on chance.'

'How in God's name did it get into your waterproof?'

'That's what I've been trying to work out. It wasn't in my pocket when we left for the service at six o'clock tonight. I'm sure about that, because going down in the car I searched through my coat for a packet of cigarettes. At some stage between that time and when I returned here at ten to eight somebody must have put it there.'

'The murderer?'

'Could be. Or an accomplice.'

Peter was staring at him. 'Alec, are you certain . . .'

'Quite certain. Nothing I did on the Whinny Knowe last night need cause you a moment's worry.'

'Is somebody trying to frame you?'

'I don't know.'

'Whom did you come in contact with, during the service and afterwards?'

121

'I've been thinking along those lines, naturally. But it's impossible to make a credible list. Going into the church I rubbed shoulders and talked with a dozen different people. The same coming out. Afterwards I was with young Isaac Semple and his wife at Ardcapple Cottage, but I'm convinced neither of them had anything to do with it.' He dropped the bracelet on the table. 'Peter,' he said, 'I need your advice. What's my next move?'

His brother went across to the fireplace. He put one elbow on the mantelpiece and stood half turned away, flicking ash from his cigarette into the dying fire.

He said: 'We're in a spot, Alec. Both of us.'

'Both?'

'Yes.'

'What d'you mean?'

'There's nothing else for it. We must go to the police first thing in the morning. Tell them the exact truth.'

'But wait a minute, Peter . . .'

'If we don't, there may be—complications. They'll keep our evidence to themselves, for the time being at any rate. Meg needn't hear about it.'

'You've been keeping something back, so as not to upset Meg?'

'I was thinking about the child as well.'

'Sure, but . . .'

'Alec, you remember the car you saw last night? On Riverside Street. You said it looked familiar.'

'Yes. I've been racking my brains, trying to remember . . .'

'You needn't any longer. It was your own Cortina. I was driving it.'

122

11

IN the morning a dank drizzle of rain blanketed Kilcolum. The sitting-room window in the Fraser Arms was blurred by condensation. As they sat facing the policemen, Peter and Alec could see little of what was going on in the street outside.

Greenless was sombre but otherwise not noticeably moved by what they had just told him. In contrast, MacKinlay leant forward against the table-edge, bright with interest and suspicion. Before him was a notebook in which he had been recording their stories.

To Peter he said: 'For anyone in your position, sir— a magistrate and a person of standing in the community —it seems incredible you should have tried to conceal your movements on the night of the murder.'

'I didn't try to conceal them. I omitted to tell you about them until now!' Peter did his best to camouflage dislike of the sergeant, but without much success. He went on: 'Even a magistrate is human. As I've tried to explain, my wife is expecting a baby. It would be bad for her if I came under suspicion and she started worrying.'

Greenlees coughed, rendering still-born another comment from his colleague. He said: 'You were wise to come to us, Mr Fraser. Certain evidence led us to suspect that the Cortina from the Big House might have been in the village on Monday night. We checked the tracks on the golf course road and found they corresponded with the pattern on its tyres. I take it,' he added, 'that if necessary your wife will confirm the times of your departure and return on the night in question?'

'She will, Inspector.'

'Then let's recapitulate. At about eight o'clock you became worried because your brother had not yet come home?'

'That's right. I rang Willie MacNaughton. He told me that Alec had spoken to him on the golf course but had then gone on to the village. I had a hunch and rang the Fraser Arms and was told by the manager that my brother had just left in the company of Dan Sillars and Dr Young. I asked to speak to young Isaac Semple, the barman. He admitted to me that Alec might have drunk more than was good for him.'

'Go on.'

Peter noticed that the sergeant was checking every word against his notes. 'It was a wet night,' he said. 'I decided, therefore, it might be a good thing if I went to meet Alec. His Cortina was parked at the front door, so I took it in preference to my own Land Rover which was in a shed at the back. I calculated that if Alec intended to come straight home he'd turn left into Fisher Row and then take the road by the golf course. In consequence, I drove along the golf course road and entered the village by way of Fisher Row. I saw no sign of him. I went on past the Fraser Arms, took a turn through the new housing-scheme, then started back by way of Riverside Street. By this time I was beginning to believe that my brother had taken the Ardcapple short-cut, using the footbridge, and might reach home before me.'

'Whereas,' interpolated MacKinlay, 'at that particular moment he was still in Craig's Wynd. That is, according to *his* evidence.'

Alec frowned. 'Dr Young, Dan Sillars and I probably spoke for several minutes outside the hotel. You know how it is when you've had a drink: time seems to pass

124

quickly.' He was surprised by his own coolness. He went on: 'As Peter drove into Main Street from Fisher Row I reckon he missed me by only a few seconds. As far as I can remember, I remained quite some time in Craig's Wynd, feeling sick and sorry for myself and being afraid in the dark. It all figures, as they say.'

The sergeant shrugged and was about to speak when Greenlees again interrupted: 'At any rate it's not impossible. Continue, Mr Fraser.'

Peter sat upright, like a soldier. This was the part he'd found difficult to tell the first time. He had to exercise all his will-power to appear unmoved as he repeated it.

'I passed Craig's Wynd on my left and saw a little girl in Brownie uniform running along Riverside Street. I slowed down and recognised her as Mary Allen. Knowing that her home was only about fifty yards ahead, I decided it wasn't worth while stopping to give her a lift. I waved to her. She waved back. Then I changed down and accelerated away towards the golf course road. Half-way along, at the usual stopping-place, I drew up for a minute to light a cigarette. I got home at about twenty-five past eight.'

His eyes were dark with pain. Alec had almost forgotten his own predicament in a burgeoning sympathy with his brother.

'My God,' said Peter, 'if only I'd stopped! If only I'd taken her with me, those few yards!'

The inspector nodded. 'Life is full of regrets, Mr Fraser. But life goes on. You have more to tell us. You saw Mary Allen on Riverside Street. And another person?'

'Yes. As I approached the old houses near the golf course I saw somebody coming towards me, on the pavement. I can't tell you if it was a man or a woman: just a dark figure which shied away from my headlights and seemed to melt into a doorway. I suspected nothing. I paid no attention. But—but I realise now it could have been the murderer.'

A sceptical look on MacKinlay's face became settled, almost permanent. 'Sounds like something out of a book, sir. In real life those mysterious dark figures don't often crop up. If they do, there's usually something about them which leads to identification. Height, build, manner of walking...'

'I've told you, Sergeant, I only caught a glimpse of this person. A kind of shadow which moved briefly in my sight and was then gone. At the time I scarcely noticed it. Now, when I try to think back, only an impression remains.'

'Would you say tall or short, stout or thin?'

'I don't know. It was about twenty or thirty yards away.'

'On Riverside Street, between Mary Allen's house and Craig's Wynd?'

'Yes.'

'It was in your headlights for only a second or two. Then it disappeared into a doorway?'

'I think so.'

'How can you be so specific about the doorway and so vague about the person?'

Yesterday Alec had depended on his brother's solid support. Today he had the feeling that their roles were reversed. Sharply he said: 'We're not all eagle-eyed sleuths like you, Sergeant MacKinlay. I know exactly how vague a memory can be. I didn't even recognise my own car, remember.'

'I remember.' The sergeant's voice was cold, almost menacing. He turned to Peter and said: 'This—this figure

126

you saw, could it have been your brother?'

'No! I keep telling you I'd have recognised my brother?'

'Even at twenty or thirty yards, in the dark, with all this melting into doorways going on?'

Ponderously, Greenlees butted in: 'Leave it there, MacKinlay. Now, let's see, Mr Fraser. You returned to Kilcolum House at twenty-five past eight. What happened then?'

'I told my wife I couldn't find Alec. She said I was fussing too much, that he'd probably found a friend and gone visiting somewhere. I was still worried but tried not to show it, for her sake. Then, shortly after nine o'clock, Miss Craig phoned from Ardcapple Farm, saying he was there.'

The inspector bowed and raised his head. 'That will be all, Mr Fraser. In the meantime, at any rate. You may go now, if you wish.'

'What about my brother?'

'We'd like to go over his story again—about the bracelet, I mean—and ask him a few further questions.'

'I should like to stay.'

'Very good, sir. I have no objection.'

The bracelet lay on the table, glinting under pendant lights.

Greenlees touched it, looked across at Alec. 'Why are you so sure this is the bracelet worn by Mary Allen the night she was killed?'

'I'm *not* sure. But why should just *any* bracelet turn up in my pocket?'

'I see your point, Mr Fraser. And when we check with Mrs Allen I suspect she'll confirm your judgment. Meanwhile, let's get the position clear. You found this in the left-hand pocket of your waterproof—when, exactly?'

'At ten minutes to eight, when I returned to Kilcolum House from Ardcapple Cottage. I heard it chink as I hung my coat on the hall-stand.'

'You're positive it wasn't there when you and your brother and sister-in-law drove down to the church at six?'

'I searched my coat for cigarettes. Both pockets were empty.'

MacKinlay looked up from his notebook. 'Incidentally,' he said, 'did you find your cigarettes?'

'Yes. In my hip pocket.'

'Odd place to put cigarettes. They'd be a bit squashed?'

'They were, Sergeant. I don't ever remember doing such a thing before.'

'You were worried, of course. Upset?'

'Quite.'

'Nervous, too. And unhappy?'

Alec nodded.

Peter glowered and butted in: 'If you'd stop trying to be smart, Sergeant MacKinlay, and lay hands on the murderer, we'd all feel a great deal better.'

Greenlees made small gestures and rumbling sounds calculated to pacify. 'Early days,' he said, steady eyes on Peter. 'As you well know, sir, a precipitate arrest may have unfortunate results. The evidence may prove to be so scanty that the charge has to be dropped. This brings discredit to the police and may do the person concerned a grave injustice.'

He turned to Alec. 'Contrary to what many people think,' he went on, 'the police are taught to be jealous of the rights of individuals. One of these rights is that a person's character and position should never be challenged publicly on suspicion alone. As a newspaperman

128

you should know that, sir.'

He paused, coughing gently. Nobody spoke. Mac-Kinlay was aware that the homily had been meant for him as much as for the others.

The inspector's shoulders heaved. He sighed and said: 'Now, Mr Fraser, according to what you say, this bracelet must have been placed in your pocket some time between your arrival at the church at approximately six-fifteen and your return to Kilcolum House at seven-fifty?'

'That's right.'

'Then, if you would, cast your mind back and go over once again the list of people to whom you spoke or who brushed against you during that period.'

'I came in contact with so many, Inspector. Especially as we went into the church.'

'Nevertheless, please try to remember.'

Alec did his best.

When the brothers had gone, MacKinlay said: 'Surely a guilty man would never have come to us with that bracelet?'

Greenlees permitted himself a small smile. 'We must remember, of course, that he may be mad enough to try a double bluff.'

'There's that, sir. But—well, I must admit I've changed my original estimate of Alec Fraser. Half his trouble seems to be sheer honesty. And lack of resolution. Extraordinary in a newspaper bloke.'

The smile broadened. 'I agree, Sergeant. I can see you and I are going to get on splendidly together.'

'I don't like his brother, though. Landowner type. Real arrogant.'

'You get used to them,' said Greenlees, obliquely.

'Now'—he picked up the bracelet—'would you like to deal with this? Take the car and have it tested for fingerprints in Stewarton right away, though I don't expect any will be found except Alec Fraser's. Then come back and question Mrs Allen about it.'

'Wilco.'

'The whole job shouldn't take you more than a couple of hours. I'll have a word with Miss Thomson myself. On the same subject.'

Grace Allen sat staring at the bracelet on her lap. The drizzle outside was lifting. Sunlight came intermittently into the bare, cheerless kitchen.

'Mary begged me to let her wear it. She was so proud, showing it to Tom and Mr Semple before she left.'

Her husband sat at the table, raw hands clasped together. He said: 'She found it in a drawer. I never even knew Grace had it.'

'Solid silver,' said MacKinlay. 'Looks valuable.'

'I—I don't know about that.' Grace looked up, almost guiltily.

'You've had it for some time?'

'Since—since before I married.'

'A present?'

She nodded, lips quivering.

'From one of her boy-friends, likely.' There was neither jealousy nor bitterness in Tom Allen's voice, only a desire to ease his wife's unhappiness with a small joke.

After a silence MacKinlay said: 'Was it from a boy-friend?'

She nodded.

'Who was he?'

She began to cry, soundlessly, tears flowing on her

130

pale full cheeks. MacKinlay discovered that his modern outlook was not, after all, impervious to sentiment. He felt like a bully. He should never have asked this woman, in the presence of her husband, for the identity of an old flame. In any case, she was bereaved and suffering from shock. His questions would have to be put more skilfully, with more sympathy and restraint.

'I know how you feel, Mrs Allen. Ancient history is usually best forgotten.'

'Yes,' she whispered. 'I want to forget.'

He took out a packet of cigarettes. She accepted one, and he lit it for her. Tom Allen said he'd have a pipe, later.

'There's just one point,' the sergeant went on, exhaling smoke. 'This locket gimmick. The lid was open. It was empty inside. Can you tell me if it ever contained anything—a picture, a lock of hair?'

'No, no. There was nothing.'

But the way she said it, the timbre of scared defiance in her voice, convinced him she was lying.

'You'd swear to that in a court of law?'

At the table Tom Allen stirred, anger in his thin unshaven face. 'She said there was nothing. She's had enough to bear without all this third degree.'

'I'm sorry, Mr Allen. I'm just trying to do my job. You want us to find the murderer, don't you?'

'Ay.' The man's anger switched from MacKinlay to the unknown killer of his child. His hands went out, clamping round a big family Bible on the table. He lifted it, let it drop. 'Ay. By God, you're right! But what's the good of questions about a bracelet?'

The sergeant could appreciate his point. Action was what Mary's father wanted, not slow and painstaking inquiry. He himself was aware that a great deal of good might come from questions about the bracelet. But it appeared that specific answers would be difficult to come by, and he simply hadn't the heart to wield his authority in this house of mourning.

Grace Allen dragged heavily on her cigarette, wiped her cheeks with the back of a grimy hand. Glancing across at him with unexpected interest and intelligence, she said: 'Where did you find it?'

'At the moment,' he told her, 'I'm not at liberty to say.'

Specimens of Alec Fraser's fingerprints had been obtained from the polished surface of the table in the hotel. In the County Headquarters lab in Stewarton they had been found repeated on the bracelet, which was otherwise clean. As yet Inspector Greenlees wouldn't commit himself, but MacKinlay's own theory was that the murderer had wiped it before dropping it into the pocket of Alec Fraser's waterproof.

To Mary's mother he said: 'You'll get the bracelet back, of course. Meanwhile we have to hold on to it. Evidence, you understand.'

She handed it back to him. She had stopped crying and was studying his face. He had the feeling that she, too, wanted to ask more questions. Something about her attitude puzzled him. Grief had been temporarily superseded by—what? Curiosity? Anxiety?

He looked at his wrist-watch. It was almost one o'clock. 'I'll be going now,' he said. 'But I may come back ...'

There was a knock at the front door. He stood by his chair, listening.

The door was opened and closed. Footsteps shuffled along the passage towards the kitchen. Old Isaac Semple came in, bowler hat in hand, overcoat open to reveal his undertaker's black suit.

He stared at the sergeant, eyes inimical, hard. 'Can't you leave them alone?' he said.

'I'm just going.'

'Your duty is to find the maniac who killed their daughter. Not to stay here snooping, smoking cigarettes.'

MacKinlay threw his stub into the old-fashioned steel range. He noticed that Grace Allen had dropped her cigarette on the tiled floor and was crushing it out with her shoe. She was crying again, her face hidden in her hands.

Tom Allen rose from the table. 'You've come about the funeral, Mr Semple?'

'Ay. I've just been talking to Inspector Greenlees. He's had a phone message from the Procurator Fiscal. The forensic man has been to Stewarton and done the post mortem. He found nothing more than the doctors did. We can go ahead now, Tom.'

'Tomorrow? Tomorrow afternoon? The sooner it's over . . .'

'God's will be done. She'll have the finest coffin in the shop, and the funeral won't cost you a penny. You've been a faithful servant to me, Tom. I don't forget.'

He saw the Bible on the table. He put his hand on it, raised his head and closed his eyes. A ray of sunlight picked out the lines and bristles on his face.

'Let us pray,' he said, the harsh voice mellowing into unction.

Obediently, Tom Allen bowed his head. Grace sobbed, took a long shuddering breath behind her hands and became still. The sergeant watched from behind lowered eyelids. He was embarrassed. He had the same feeling about spontaneous prayer as about spontaneous love-making: unsuspecting citizens had a right to be protected from it. But he stayed and listened all the same.

Apparently plucking inspiration from the low ceiling, Isaac Semple made a groaning sound and continued: 'O Lord, give Thy servants strength to bear their burden. Fill their hearts with the knowledge that their daughter died according to Thy will. Comfort them now, O Lord, and bless the purpose of Thine elect. Glory be to the Father, Son and Holy Ghost, world without end. Amen.'

He opened his eyes and saw that MacKinlay was still present. Instantly religious fervour was transmuted into anger. 'Get out!' he commanded. 'There is nothing for you here. Have you no questions to ask of the strangers in Kilcolum? The libertines, the fornicators?'

MacKinlay had had enough. He lifted his coat from the back of a chair and went.

As he walked along Riverside Street and into Fisher Row, heading for the hotel, his embarrassed annoyance soon faded and he found himself inclined to giggle. He felt guilty about it, remembering the death of Mary Allen. But old Semple was a unique character in his experience. He'd heard of the type, the calvinistic Scot convinced of his own righteousness, of his special worth in the eyes of God, but this was the first time he'd met a living example. The sepulchral clothes, the unctuous voice, the 'wrath of God' face, they were almost incredible against the background of a modern permissive society. The man was a throw-back, a creature to be pitied, too, like a plesiosaurus in Loch Ness. Kilcolum, a country backwater far from what might be called civilisation, was, of course, the natural habitat of such a man.

The sergeant allowed himself a laugh and a shake of the head. Then he forgot about Isaac Semple and the fervour of his prayer.

134

12

THE *Stewarton Echo,* circulation 5000, had a new editor, a young man called Jock MacNiven who'd served his apprenticeship in the BBC newsroom in Glasgow. A murder on his doorstep, so to speak, was manna from heaven. His labours of the previous afternoon and evening were now proclaimed in giant headlines. Examples from the popular dailies included SEX FIEND STRIKES and MANIAC STALKS THE MOOR. The more sober prints contented themselves with such as MYSTERIOUS DEATH OF A SCHOOLGIRL and POLICE INVESTIGATE BROWNIE MURDER.

Jock's activities resulted in the precipitate arrival in the district by car, plane and helicopter, not only of special writers and photographers from the press but also of cameramen and reporters from television. He'd made a financial killing the first day. Now he was faced with overwhelming competition and leaner times. It was an occupational hazard.

Nevertheless, following a tradition in local journalism, he gave his colleagues from the outside world a warm welcome and organised their accommodation in various hotels in Stewarton and in the Fraser Arms in Kilcolum. He also persuaded Inspector Greenlees that the best way of disciplining such a mob of news-hungry men and women was to hold a twice-daily press conference. The first was arranged for five o'clock that afternoon in the Fraser Arms.

The sitting-room was crowded long before the stated time. When the inspector and MacKinlay came in, Jock straightened his tie, smoothed down his umkempt black

135

hair, and introduced them to his fellow tradesmen in a manner calculated to keep him on good terms with everybody.

There were many questions. Tape-recorders whined. Cameras clicked and whirred and flashed. Inspector Greenlees was unperturbed but exceedingly careful. His answers, though sometimes long and weighty, could be condensed and summarised into the statement that the investigation was proceeding and an early arrest expected.

Brashly, the *Express* said: 'So you think you know who did it?'

'The evidence,' said Greenlees, 'is beginning to point in a certain direction. I have just been talking to the Procurator Fiscal in Stewarton. He agrees.'

'This maniac angle,' put in the *Scotsman*. 'Does it stand up?'

'Possibly.'

The *Courier* was a lank-haired young woman with sex appeal smothered by a bulky anorak, thick grey ski-pants and Wellington boots. She said, eagerly: 'In that case, are there liable to be more murders?'

'Not if we can help it,' replied the inspector, with solid calm.

When? Where? How? It was like rain on a corrugated iron roof, thought MacKinlay.

He was under orders to say nothing unless specifically requested to do so by the inspector. He was glad of this. He was beginning to have considerable respect for his superior not only as a policeman but as a shrewd public relations man. In this respect, especially after the ticking off he'd endured from Greenlees for his conduct of the interview with Grace Allen, he realised he had a lot to learn. He wasn't looking forward to going back to the

Allen house to ask the proper questions. This interlude of comparative obscurity under the wing of the inspector was just what he needed to compose his mind and re-orientate his thoughts.

The conference broke up at a quarter to six.

The pressmen scattered to try to secure 'quotes' from people connected with the case—the Allens and their relatives the MacKays, Dr Young and Dan Sillars, Jenny Craig and Kate Thomson, Peter and Alec Fraser.

Particularly Peter and Alec Fraser. A local laird was traditionally a profitable source of 'copy', while a well-known feature writer on holiday was a gift to gimmick-conscious reporters. And wasn't there the hint of a rumour that Alec Fraser was actually under suspicion?

They also wanted to ask Isaac Semple about the funeral and Archie Craig about his 'strangled' sheep.

On the whole they were pessimistic about getting helpful answers from anybody. In their opinion the inhabitants of remote places like Kilcolum were like clams when it came to a murder case. Inbreeding was usually the cause of the trouble.

MacKinlay had a pint of strong ale with Jock Mac-Niven in the public bar, where they talked mainly about ancient gossip concerning the death of Nancy MacKay. Then he joined the inspector in the dining-room for their evening meal.

As he ate the last of his cheese and washed it down with a draught of strong black coffee, Greenlees said: 'You must get it out of her, MacKinlay. By crook if not by normal hook. The jeweller in Stewarton remembers selling that bracelet six years ago. He's prepared to identify the buyer in court.'

'I'll do it, sir. Sorry I let sentiment and religion dull my brain this morning.'

'We're always learning,' said Greenlees, sententiously.

While the conference had been taking place, Meg was lying down after finishing her household chores and putting a joint in the oven for dinner. She felt quite fit and unencumbered by the child in her womb, but Peter kept looking at her with such sad and anxious eyes that in order to please him she had agreed to rest for an hour.

There was something odd about Peter, a kind of tender secrecy which wasn't like him. Resolutely she put it down to his concern for her in this environment of murder-talk. He had been out searching for Alec on the night of the murder, but that of course could only be a coincidence. No doubt he was worried also about Alec's position.

Everything would resolve itself soon, she told herself, when the police discovered the truth. Men were inclined to be neurotic, assailed by sophisticated fears which seldom troubled women, who had more elementary problems to worry about. For instance, she herself would be very relieved when Mrs MacKay returned after the funeral and the functioning of the house returned to normal.

She dismissed incipient doubt from her mind and tried to sleep.

Peter came in from the fields where he had been helping one of his hired hands to clear a choked petrol-feed in a tractor. He had also been having a look at his black-face ewes on the lower ground. The first cross-bred lambs were due in the next fortnight, and a careful eye had to be kept on the mothers-to-be.

He found his brother in the study reading Jock Mac-Niven's contributions to the *Express* and *Scotsman*. which had arrived by post less than an hour ago.

He said: 'Have a drink, Alec. Pour me a stiff one, too.'

'Feeling tired?'

'A bit. This murder, it's getting me down.'

'We're all in the same boat.' Alec handed him a bountiful whisky and added water. He topped his own small ration with soda and raised his glass. 'Here's hoping Greenlees and MacKinlay do a quick, clean job.'

Peter swallowed, coughed, lit a cigarette. 'They're on to that bracelet. I have a feeling.'

'Its origin and history, you mean?'

'Yes.'

'Well, I hope they are, if it points to the murderer.'

'It points to me, Alec.'

Outside on the lawn blackbirds had been calling to each other as the sun went down. Now heavy clouds were rolling up again, and they were quiet.

Peter said: 'Switch on the light and draw the curtains.'

Alec did so. He went and stood by the fire and looked down at Peter, slumped in a leather armchair. He said: 'What are you trying to tell me?'

'We're up against it, you and I. What's the Latin tag? "The sins we commit as young men we pay for in old age." '

'All right, Peter. We're practically strangers in a sense, but we're still brothers. We tell each other the truth and face up to it together.'

'Sure. It's Meg I keep thinking about. She's so young. She—she depends on me. "Old Reliable" she calls me.'

'Well?'

He gulped down the remainder of his whisky. He said: 'I gave that bracelet to Nancy MacKay. Six years ago.'

Alec took a long drag at his cigarette. 'For services rendered?'

'You could put it like that. God, you'll hate me for what I did!'

'I told you things about myself last night that made your hair curl. You didn't disown me.'

'But my story has nothing *big* about it. It's merely pathetic.'

'Tell me just the same.'

Peter nodded: 'She came to work here when she was about eighteen. She was—very attractive. Not long after Father died, Mother took ill. Remember? You'd just gone to London. She was in bed for weeks. I was a bit off colour myself, worried about her and about the estate. One Sunday I gave the housekeeper and the nurse an afternoon and evening off. Nancy and I had a lot of fun working together, looking after Mother, cooking the meals. Not long after I'd gone to bed that night she came to my room in her nightgown, apparently very frightened. A sound at her bedroom window, she said. I went to investigate. There was nothing.'

'And you stayed?'

Peter nodded. 'It was the first of several times. I was over thirty, Alec. I'd never had a woman before. She was all fire and magic.'

'Then you discovered you weren't her only flame?'

Peter's spaniels lay on the hearth-rug. He looked up and his eyes were like theirs, questioning, appealing. 'I heard about her romance with young Isaac Semple. Dan Sillars told me several stories about the Mackay women, suggesting they were nymphomaniacs and gold-diggers.' He put a hand to his forehead. 'But Nancy wasn't like that. Not really. She lived for the moment. The night I gave her the bracelet she cried on my shoulder. Then she—she repaid me, more passionately than ever before.'

'Go on,' said Alec.

'There's not much else to tell. That's why I said my story is pathetic. As far as I'm concerned it ended tamely. I wakened up from a dream, in one way relieved, in another disappointed. We—we lost interest in each other. My fault, I expect. Mother died, and I had so many other problems to cope with. Next thing I knew the tale was going round that Nancy was in the family way and that young Isaac was responsible.'

'By that time she'd left here?'

'Yes. She'd had a row with the housekeeper and gone to work at Cuthbert's, the grocery store in the village. Then—then it happened. She was found dead in the burn. I—I don't think I was to blame for her condition, Alec. She never said a word to me.'

'D'you reckon she told anybody? About what happened between you?'

'I'm almost certain she didn't. This is another characteristic of the MacKay women—extreme loyalty to their boy-friends. Don't ask me to explain it, Alec. Maybe they think along the same lines as men do. They take their pleasure from us. When it's over they're satisfied, grateful. Mum's the word. Honour among thieves.'

'I don't believe that's so unusual. In women, I mean. When it comes to the bit women are far better at keeping a secret than men. At least, in my experience.' Alec looked hard at his brother. 'Did anyone suspect what was going on?' he asked.

Peter shook his head, 'At that time Dan Sillars was always giving me lectures about the MacKays and how dangerous they were, and he may have suspected something. I'm not sure, either, about Nancy's mother.' He paused. Then, almost urgently, he went on: 'In a way I loved that girl, Alec. Given a chance she could have made something of her life. But Kilcolum and her family

141

history, they were too much for her. I didn't help, either. She died. I gave her mother a job here—a good job with much above the average wages. Conscience, I expect. It always works too late.'

Alec noted the bitterness and said, quietly: 'You told me about Nancy's death almost as soon as I got here? Why?'

'I was afraid you might mention it to Mrs MacKay. That would have hurt her. What she told you might also have given you ideas about me.'

'I'm not with you.'

'She's always on about how happy Nancy was in the Big House. How she even preferred to sleep here rather than at home. You might have jumped to the proper conclusions. Anyway, I'm not sure how much Mrs Mac-Kay knows. Sometimes she looks at me as if we shared a secret.'

'I see.' Alec found it difficult to appreciate the argument, but he tried to make allowances for his brother's anxious and therefore slightly confused state of mind. 'I'm glad you've told me about it now,' he went on. 'You're not to blame for Nancy's death, of course, but in a way your position is much the same as mine. There's a residual guilt complex.'

'And something else, Alec. Something else that always worries me.'

'The bracelet?'

'I don't mean only the bracelet. What I can't bring myself to believe is that Nancy committed suicide. She wasn't the type at all. She was happy-go-lucky, extrovert, taking life at it came and usually enjoying it. In any case, I'm sure she'd never have killed herself simply because she was going to have a baby. She'd have taken

142

the so-called "disgrace" in her stride and made somebody pay for it.'

Alec dropped his cigarette into the fire, took a sip
from his glass. 'You inferred that the MacKays, including Nancy, were loyal to their boy-friends. In that case,
how did the rumour about young Isaac start?'

'I don't know. Nancy was very friendly with Mrs
MacNaughton, Willie's mother. The old lady may have
put two and two together, dropped a hint to somebody.'

A peat in the fireplace dissolved into hissing ash. One
of the spaniels stirred and snored in his sleep.

'Now,' said Alec, 'about the bracelet.'

'I bought it in Stewarton. At MacBrayne's the jewel-
lers. Greenlees is bound to find out.'

'Only a few hours ago you had the chance to give him
this information. Why didn't you?'

'I was ashamed, afraid.'

'Then hadn't you better make a clean breast of it
now, before he decides to question you again?'

'He—he might arrest me. What would happen to
Meg?'

'He won't arrest you. He's got far too many slick
answers. You, for one. Me, for another. But he knows
that you and I weren't the only people abroad in Kilcolum at the time of the murder. I could mention two
myself: Dan Sillars and the doctor. When I left them
outside the Fraser Arms that night they both intended
to walk home, Dan because he hadn't got his car, Jimmy
Young because he was afraid to risk a breathalyser test.
There were others, too—many others, in fact.

'And I should imagine Greenlees will want to be certain about a motive before he starts arresting anybody.
There's the maniac angle, of course. That might tend
to implicate me, especially after my performances in

London. But I don't think even Sergeant MacKinlay would suspect you of going batty at every full moon and assaulting little girls. And another thing. You gave the bracelet to Nancy. How did it come to be in Grace Allen's possession?'

'Nancy may have given it to her.'

'That doesn't sound like a MacKay.'

'It may have been among her effects. I mean, when she died.'

'Grace was only her cousin. Surely all Nancy's effects would go to her mother?'

Alec's cool reason was having an effect. More calmly, Peter said: 'I didn't think of that.' He lit another cigarette. He frowned and said: 'Look, you do believe me, don't you?'

'It all rings true to me. And it has reinforced my opinion that there's something ugly and evil going on in Kilcolum. Talk about a maniac points to me. Now the bracelet points to you. Somebody's raising a smokescreen, but I don't think Greenlees will allow much of the smoke to get in his eyes.'

'I'll tell him in the morning.'

'Why not tonight?'

'You're going out to see Willie.'

'Yes, but . . .'

'I'll stay with Meg. Old Reliable. With all those damned reporters swanning around she'll need protection. Anyway, it may not be necessary to tell him after all. By tomorrow he may have discovered the murderer.'

Alec was about to describe this as false optimism when they heard Meg coming downstairs.

'Not a word,' Peter warned him.

She came into the study, humming a gentle tune.

144

'Come on, you Fraser oafs! If you want any dinner come and help me!'

In the kitchen, busy at the stove, she began humming the tune again. Recognising it, Alec shivered. It was *Hebridean Cradle Song*, the voluntary he had heard in church.

13

BEFORE and during dinner Peter had to deal with newsmen on the phone and newsmen at the front door. His temper became short, and Meg, with potatoes and mutton gravy turning cold, nagged back in frustration.

Eventually, Alec took over. He spoke to the journalists as one of themselves, keeping them happy with unimportant snippets of local colour but letting it be known firmly that he and his brother had nothing at all to say about the murder. Playing a final card, he told them that young Mrs Fraser was expecting a baby, that she was without her daily help and therefore entitled to a peaceful evening. The toughest of reporters is a sentimentalist at heart. Without exception they agreed to lay off Kilcolum House, for the time being at any rate.

'Just one more question,' said the *Courier*, standing with her Wellington boots planted wide apart in front of the study fire. 'Would you say there's any connection between this murder and the death of Mary Allen's second cousin, Nancy MacKay, six years ago?'

Alec felt slightly sick. He disciplined his expression,

however, and willed his eyes to remain steady. 'I have no idea. How did this occur to you?'

'Something Inspector Greenlees said at the conference.' The *Courier* brushed back swinging hair. Some of her colleagues were already on their feet, pocketing notebooks, collecting cameras. 'I understand it happened soon after your mother died. Nancy MacKay's death, I mean.'

'That's right.'

'You were here for your mother's funeral?'

'Yes. I came from London.'

'Was Nancy MacKay still employed by your brother at that time?'

'I'm not sure. Frankly I don't remember. What's the point of all this?'

'I don't know if there *is* a point. You should understand. We ask all sorts of questions, then something jells.'

The *Scotsman* said: 'She's like that, Mr Fraser. Nothing she enjoys more than teaching her elders and betters how to suck eggs!'

They parted friends, with a murmur of subdued laughter in the hall.

Returning to the dining-room, Alec assured Meg and Peter that they were unlikely to be disturbed again that night, at any rate by the press. Peter grew more relaxed. Meg chattered.

As they reached the coffee stage she approached a subject that had been in her mind all day—the relationship between Alec and Jenny Craig.

At the party the previous night her feminine eye had spotted their awareness of each other. She had been worried by Jenny's sudden decision to go upstairs while Alec was there. She remembered as a small girl over-

146

hearing adult gossip about a dance and about the laird's younger son vanishing from the Hall with Archie Craig's daughter. Was it possible that a spark of something remained between them? She hoped not. Her father was in love with Jenny, and a sensible, clever wife was just what he needed to keep him happy and on the rails of common sense and sobriety. It would be a tragedy for all concerned if anything happened to upset his hopes —and hers. Not for the first time since her marriage Meg discovered that a romantic view of the world and the people in it contained seeds of disillusionment. Everything wasn't black and white. She was beginning to admit to herself the existence of many shades of grey.

Smiling, however, and with a show of banter, she ventured an opinion. 'Don't kid me, Alec! I bet you had dozens of girls at the University!'

'I hadn't, you know. I was very studious.'

'Not even during the holidays, here in Kilcolum?'

'I was much keener on poaching than on girls. With Willie.' He was embarrassed and determined to slide off the subject. 'Willie used to be a genius at taking fish from the burn. He taught me all the angles—fly, worm, gaff, net, even the snigger. I could write a treatise on poaching if anyone would publish it.'

'Yes, but you went to dances, didn't you?'

'Oh, sure. I've had my moments!' He grinned at her and began to scatter a false trail. 'Good thing for Peter I was away when you grew up. I'd have given him a run for his money.'

'I had plenty of opposition as it was,' said Peter, touching his wife's hand. 'I had to rescue her from a horde of long-haired hippies ...'

'Darling, you *hadn't*!' She was pleased and flattered, already inclined to forget the cause of her concern. 'I may look modern, but I'm a sedate old thing inside. Sometimes it occurs to me I'm far more sedate than my husband!'

The telephone rang.

'I'll get it,' said Alec. 'If it's another reporter I'll blast his head off.'

It wasn't a reporter. It was Jenny.

'Alec, thank goodness you answered! I want to see you.'

'Right now?'

'Down by the bridge in about half an hour. Can you make it?'

'Yes, but . . .'

'Oh, Alec, last night was a mistake.' Tears blurred her voice. 'I want to explain.'

He experienced a quick lightness of heart, an onset of relief which he tried to persuade himself was simply happy anticipation of their meeting. He said: 'It's not the end of the world, Jenny. I'll be there.'

He finished his coffee and had a cigarette. Then he told Peter and Meg he must be on his way to Willie's place. 'I'll walk,' he said, casually. 'It's pretty dark outside, but at least the rain has kept off.'

Peter said: 'If we're in bed by the time you get back, see to the windows and lock the front door, will you?'

He took the short-cut, through the trees below the house, across the big field which had once shone with barley. Playing coy among drifting rafts of clouds, a young moon gave him enough light to see only a few yards ahead. But bright windows in Ardcapple Farm and in the cottage guided him on to the road and towards the bridge.

He stopped near the concrete steps rising to the long

148

wooden span. Jenny had not yet come. There was a light wind, furtive and almost silent.

Small rustlings occurred on the river-bank. Water tinkled among loose stones. Alec could feel the smell of damp earth and grass, of tar from the looming bridge. It reminded him of nights with Willie, crouched on the burnside with torch and net, waiting for a swirl in the water that would betray the onrush of a salmon, while excitement seethed inside him and made him cold. The same kind of excitement possessed him now.

He lit a cigarette, not only to ease his nerves but also because its glow would signal his presence to Jenny.

Above the river, on the other side, the village looked like a liner at anchor, its portholes gleaming. Cars moved on the streets, faintly whining, their headlights stabbing on as they moved out on to the open, unlit roads.

Something splashed into the burn below the bridge. His flesh crawled. He told himself not to be a craven idiot. A water-rat, perhaps. A piece of loose earth disturbed by a burrowing mole. A small trout leaping to avoid a cannibal neighbour. Country sounds were mysterious only to townsfolk. At one time they'd conveyed news to him, not ignorant fears. But he'd lived for so long as an urbanite, his ears tuned to political whispering, that he'd lost the ability to interpret them.

He was aware of her scent before he heard her footsteps on the verge of the road. He moved to meet her.

She came and laid a hand on one lapel of his waterproof. 'Alec, what must you think of me?'

'I think you're beautiful.' He threw away his cigarette, took her hand and held it against his chest. 'I could take you in my arms now ...'

'Please, we're not children any more. I loved you, Alec. When you—when you went away I kept on loving

149

you. I waited for years, hoping that a dream might come true, but then—then I heard rumours about what happened in London. It came to me that I really meant nothing to you. When I thought it out I decided I'd simply been romantic, in love with an idea of love.'

It sounded like a speech that had been rehearsed. Perhaps it was.

'So Dan asked you to marry him, and you said yes?'

'Dan is in love with me. He's a fine man. He was born with a chip on his shoulder. In a country community like Kilcolum, so conservative, so feudal in a way, many people called him a misfit. But he's just being honest with himself. His—his first wife didn't help. She could talk about nothing that interested him, books, the school, social problems. She thought him bad-tempered, taciturn, told everybody what a hard life she had with him. Oh, I know I shouldn't say it, but she *drove* him to drink. He found some consolation in watching Meg grow up, beautiful and eager, marrying Peter. But now that he's alone again . . .' She broke off, struggling to control her breath.

'Are you in love with him, Jenny?'

She moved even closer. 'Alec, please understand. I'll be happy with Dan. He'll rage and bluster and enjoy himself, trying unsuccessfully to put the world to rights. I'll look after his house and his comfort and be glad that he loves me and depends on me so much. You see, I—I'm not a young girl any more with stars in my eyes. I'm almost middle-aged. Security is important.'

She pressed her cheek against his coat. She gave a little sob and said: 'I told you last night I loved you. In a way it's true. If you insisted, I'd give myself to you now, go away with you tomorrow. But it wouldn't work out. When—when we kissed last night I was feeling sorry

150

for you. Well, not so much sorry as angry at all the gossip being bandied about, at the idea that anybody could ever suspect you of—of having harmed a woman or a child. You're not made that way. You're kind. You couldn't be ruthless if you tried. I found myself involved in your sadness and anxiety, wanting to show you I was on your side. Anyway, I had been drinking.'

She was talking fast, her arms about him, her face hidden. He was trembling. She was asking for help, for guidance and release. He willed himself to stay calm.

'Not all that much,' he whispered.

'The trouble is I scarcely ever drink.' She looked up. He saw an appeal flare in her eyes. 'Something happened to me. I forgot Dan. I started to remember that time in the field over there. I wanted you to hold me, to feel your hands on my body, to recapture the desire and the affection. But—oh, Alec, it's no use.' She looked away again and hid her face. 'There's more to life than just physical excitement. When I came to myself this morning I knew it was all wrong—I mean, that we should love each other. I couldn't make you happy. I—I'd always be so afraid.'

'Afraid?'

'That when our bodies were appeased nothing would be left. It's different with Dan. We'll find contentment simply in being part of Kilcolum. You've got to face life as it is, Alec, not as you dream about it.'

The moon ducked behind a cloud, causing a moment of darkness. A movement occurred on the far bank. They were so absorbed in each other that neither of them heard it.

Alec knew that Jenny's argument was sensible and right. He, too, had been living with an ideal given spurious life by memory and imagination. The guilt factor in

151

his illness had probably been created in part by comparisons between the innocence of his affection for Jenny and the crudeness of his desire for Elizabeth. Like Jenny, though he had struggled against admitting it, he was sure now that their kisses the previous night had torn the tinsel from romance, making it evident that something was missing.

He said: 'I never thought as much of you as I do now.'

She drew in her breath, stirred and stood apart from him, though her fingers continued to clutch his coat. 'I've worked it out,' she said. 'We're too much like each other, with the same weaknesses. We need somebody to buttress those weakness, to give us confidence, to make us less vulnerable. Dan is my buttress. You will find yours, I hope. But we have strength in other ways, Alec. We—we're using it now.'

'You're a wonderful person, Jenny.'

'I could have told you all this in a letter. I'm such a coward I started to do it that way. But then—then I knew I'd have to see you to make certain you don't think I'm deserting you, when you're in all this trouble.' The moon came out again. She smiled at him, shakily. 'I know everything will turn out well for you. The police are bound to find the murderer. You're not to be sad, Alec.'

He caught her to him. She made no effort to resist, and he held her there, his cheek against her hair. 'Thank you,' he said. And after a time: 'Did Dan suspect what happened last night?'

'Yes. I'm going to see him now. I owe him the truth. He'll understand.'

He kissed her and tasted the salt of her tears. He had no desire at the moment to analyse his feelings, but had

152

he tried to do so he might have found it difficult. A sense of relief tangled with a knowledge of loss.

'Don't be sad,' she said again. 'You need somebody to—to believe in you, to show you affection, to love you. I know. I'm like that, too. Sometimes it seems as if nobody cares, as if you're unpopular and out of step with the whole world. But it's just a malaise, which passes. People who appear to be cruel and aloof suddenly become friendly. The change isn't in them but in you. If you need reassurance, Alec, be sure you can aways come to me. I believe in you. I—I like you. So does Dan. So does the doctor. Be yourself, Alec. Don't be sad or suspicious or afraid.'

'Oh, Jenny. It could have turned out so differently.'

She knew what he meant. His mind and his body were losing discipline. Abruptly she kissed him and thrust herself back and away.

They parted. She moved towards the bridge, her shadowy figure merging with and disappearing in the dark. He stood there motionless, listening to her climbing the steps, walking lightly along the high span. Presently he would go in the same direction and on the other side take the road which led to the golf course and Willie the Bomber's house. Why hadn't he accompanied her across the bridge? It would have meant a casual anticlimax, a spoliation of their mood, something neither of them could have borne with equanimity.

His ears told him that by now she had reached the other side. Over and over in his mind a verse of Burns was turning: *'Had we never lov'd sae kindly, Had we never lov'd sae blindly, Never met—or never parted, We had ne'er been broken-hearted.'* Neither of them was broken-hearted, but it was always hard to relinquish a dream and face the day.

153

Jenny screamed. Involuntarily, he uttered a small cry of alarm.

She screamed again, on a rising pitch of horror. He ran, leaping up the steps, shoes rattling at speed on the planking. White rails swam past on either side. There were sounds on the far bank, a thudding and a stamping, and Jenny's screams continuing, choking, becoming weaker, stabbing in his head like red-hot rivets.

'Jenny!' he called, jumping and slipping down the far steps.

He was conscious of heaving shadows on the little path between the bridge and Riverside Street, of a stir and commotion on the street itself. Then his heel encountered a concrete projection. He lost balance. Arms flailing in the dark he fell, jarring knee and elbow on the hard ground.

He got up, limping but otherwise unhindered by the pain. Stumbling forward, he found her lying in a heap on the path, moaning.

He knelt down, cradled her head and shoulders in his arms. Her forehead was bleeding.

'Jenny, what happened?'

One hand scrabbled at her throat, demonstrating. Moonlight flickered. Peering close he saw that her blouse was torn and that red weals necklaced her flesh.

'Who was it?' he said.

She coughed, muttered thickly: 'Hands behind me, round my throat. I struggled. We fell.'

'Did you recognise—whoever it was?'

She shook her head, stiffly, painfully. She tried to move closer, to hide against him.

Running feet on the path, approaching. Men's voices.

Alec looked up. He saw Sergeant MacKinlay looking down at him. Beside the policeman was Dan Sillars.

154

14

WILLIE opened the door. 'Man, Alec, I was starting to believe you werena coming.'

As he hung his waterproof in the hall he saw on a neighbouring peg a woman's anorak and heard voices in the sitting-room. 'Visitors?' he said.

'No' exactly. It's Miss Kate. I asked her to come.' Willie avoided Alec's eyes. 'But here,' he went on, quickly, 'you're no' looking so well. Has something happened?'

'I'll tell you in a minute.'

The heat in the sitting-room suited old bones but threatened to film the foreheads of others with sweat. The curtained windows were closed, and the air inside was heavy with peat-scent. An ancient wag-at-the-wa' clock above the mantelpiece showed the time to be after nine.

In a rocking-chair by the fire sat Mrs MacNaughton, wrinkled, bright-eyed, her scant white hair pulled tightly but not very effectively into a bun at the back. In honour of her visitor she had put on the black dress she'd worn in church the previous night. It was anything but fashionable, long and full in the skirt, its tight bodice almost completely hidden by a plain grey cardigan.

Opposite her, in a modern chair with wooden arm-rests, was Kate Thomson, as bright-eyed as her hostess, her face flushed by the heat, a close-fitting pastel-blue jumper and dark blue slacks indicating the slim strength of her body. She looked fresh, younger than her age. But as Alec came in, he saw that she was wary of him, anxious and even unhappy.

He and Willie took seats on a worn and faded sofa between the chairs.

'Sorry I'm late, Mrs MacNaughton. There was—an accident.'

'Och, poor Mr Alec!'

'Not to myself. Not an accident at all, in fact. An assault on Jenny Craig.'

Kate's eyes widened, searching his.

Willie said, fearfully: 'This—this maniac again?'

'I don't know. Thank God she wasn't too badly hurt.'

The old lady had stopped rocking in her chair. 'Tell us, son,' she said.

He looked up from a study of his hands. His decision was almost immediate. He was over with half-truths, with social evasions to preserve his image as the laird's brother. Willie and his mother were old friends. Kate was a new one, but in her presence he found courage to be honest. Wryly he remembered how well she had trained him in this respect.

He explained in exact detail, therefore, why he had gone to meet Jenny.

Mrs MacNaughton nodded. 'It was a nine days' wonder in Kilcolum at the time,' she said. 'How you'd left her home from the dance. But the dreams of a boy and girl are apt to change as the years go by. There's nothing to be ashamed of in that.'

Kate looked unhappy no longer. Her anxiety was still there, but now she could meet his eyes without flinching.

He hurried on, telling how he and Jenny had parted, how he'd heard her scream.

'I was holding her in my arms,' he said, 'when Sergeant MacKinlay came along, with Dan Sillars. Jenny

156

had phoned Dan to say she wanted to see him at his flat, and apparently he decided to come and meet her. As he crossed Riverside Street he heard her scream. He ran forward and bumped into MacKinlay hurrying in the same direction. Seems the sergeant had been at the Allens' and was returning to the hotel.'

'They found you there, alone wi' her.' Willie was frowning. 'Did they think you'd done it?'

'I'm not sure. MacKinlay kept looking at me in an odd kind of way. Dan was cursing and swearing and too eager to get Jenny home to worry much about anything else.'

Crisply, Kate said: 'Didn't she see anything at all of whoever attacked her?'

'The attack came from behind. She told MacKinlay she was sure it was a man, a big man with powerful hands.'

'How did you get her home?' inquired Mrs Mac-Naughton.

'After a bit she felt able to walk. Mrs Craig put her to bed and Archie phoned for the doctor. Jimmy Young happened to be out, but he must have come in soon afterwards, because he arrived at Ardcapple in less than half an hour. He says the bruising on Jenny's neck is superficial and will soon disappear. She's suffering slightly from shock, of course, but he's sure a good night's sleep will put her right. He and Dan are still at Ardcapple. MacKinlay and I came away.'

'It's a wonder Sergeant MacKinlay didn't arrest you on the spot,' Willie said. 'He's a mean-looking character.'

'He had every right to be suspicious, finding me there with Jenny and nobody else around.'

'But there *was* somebody else around,' said Kate, leaning forward, chin on hands, as if communing with herself.

Alec looked uneasy. 'Oh, you mean Dan?' he said, then shrugged. 'Luckily he was. Luckily, too, Jenny said that while she was being attacked she heard me calling and running across the bridge. That made Sergeant MacKinlay stop and think.' He paused, before adding: 'What puzzles me is why anybody should want to hurt Jenny.'

Kate said: 'It doesn't puzzle me, Alec. Somebody is trying to frame you. You happened to be near the spot on the night of the murder. So the bracelet was put into your pocket. Then Jenny was attacked soon after you were with her. If she hadn't been able to say she heard you coming it might have been the last straw as far as the police were concerned.'

'I know.' Alec frowned. 'But it all seems so crude, so naive.'

'Whoever killed Mary Allen may have just that kind of mind.' She was eager now, thoughts fully concentrated on the need to help him. 'I see the murderer as a social rebel, someone who has never come to terms with an imperfect world, someone who is angry, not because he's a misfit but because he believes all the rest of us are misfits.'

Alec and Willie glanced at each other.

Alec said: 'The police are not fools. They'll find him.'

'What if they don't? What if there's too much delay and he tries something else? How did Jimmy Young put it last night? "If somebody goes on killing to cover up his tracks, isn't that person devoid of ordinary human feeling? In other words a maniac?" This is what the murderer is doing, trying to cover up his tracks. If he

158

thinks he's being cornered he may do something even more desperate.'

'But that's just it.' Willie's normal expression, lugubriously serene, had grown ugly with anxiety. 'Why should we go meddling, ordinary folk like us? It's a job for the police, as Alec says.'

'Ordinary folk are involved with justice. Alec will be in danger until the murderer is flushed out and caught. So the sooner he's flushed out the better, and I reckon my plan will do it.'

Willie sighed. 'What a lassie!' he muttered and looked at Alec with an air of 'I told you so!'

A cold tremor rippled in the muscles of Alec's chest. 'Before we go any farther,' he said, 'I'd like to ask Mrs MacNaughton some questions about Nancy MacKay. Especially about her relationship with young Isaac Semple.'

'As many as you like,' said the old lady.

'First of all, there's the problem of that bracelet. I can't tell you exactly how I found out, but I happen to know that originally it belonged to Nancy. Perhaps Mrs MacNaughton can tell us how Grace Allen came to own it?'

Both Kate and Willie were staring at him.

Kate said: 'She can. This is what we were talking about before you came. It's the basis of my plan.'

'I'm sorry, Alec.' Willie looked more anxious than ever. 'Did Peter tell you?'

'Yes. But I thought ...'

'It's a secret wi' us, son. Nancy told my mother. She told her a lot o' things.'

Mrs MacNaughton resumed her gentle rocking, lips sucked in so much that she appeared to be toothless. 'I kept it a secret, up till now,' she said at last. 'Even

159

from Willie. It was Miss Kate here got it out of me, asking so many questions. She's that keen to help you, son.'

'Peter's going to the police in the morning.'

'Well, that's a blessing,' said Willie. 'It'll maybe put them on the right track.'

'It's Meg he's so worried about. With the baby coming...'

'He should be worried about his brother, too,' said Kate, with vigour. 'Anyway, if the plan comes off Meg need be none the wiser.'

Willie sighed again and shook his head. 'It's a dangerous business. If we've made a mistake . . .'

'If we've made a mistake,' she said, 'the police will hear about it. We'll confess and explain our actions. They'll understand. Especially Inspector Greenlees. If we haven't made a mistake—well, the person concerned will appear at the rendezvous and our suspicions will be confirmed.'

'Miss Kate is right,' said Mrs MacNaughton.

'Willie,' said Alec, 'will you please tell me what all this is about?'

At half-past ten Kate finished her cup of tea and said she would have to go. Her brother would become anxious if she stayed out too late.

Willie got up, stiffly. 'I'm getting so old, Alec. Maybe you could take over my duties and see Miss Kate home to the Manse.'

'I can manage by myself,' she said.

Alec wanted to smile. He didn't. 'It's a dark night,' he pointed out. 'Since Willie is so decrepit I must insist on being your escort.'

'As you wish.'

Mrs MacNaughton had no inhibitions. Accepting with

a broad smile their thanks for her hospitality, she shook hands with her guests and sat rocking as they left the room.

Willie helped them don anorak and waterproof.

Aware of Kate's determined and slightly aloof expression, Alec said: 'I hope you soon recover your health and strength, Willie.'

'Och, well . . .'

'I use Sloan's Liniment for rheumatism myself. Good night.'

'Good night,' said Willie. Then a beam dawned on his face. 'Man, that's more like yourself! Am I no' glad!' he called after them, waving at the door.

They were only a few yards from the house, turning on to the golf course road, when unexpectedly Kate laughed. 'He's rather a pet, isn't he?'

'Willie? A conniving rogue. Always was.'

'You're very fond of each other?'

'Buddies, as he puts it. We were poachers together. What's the old song? *"Comrades in the hour of danger."* But he taught me a lot more than how to catch a salmon illegally. The meaning of friendship, for example. Simple loyalty, with no strings attached. I'd trust my life with Willie. I believe he'd do the same with me.'

'That's a wonderful thing to say.'

'I don't know. It's true, anyway.'

'You're feeling much better, Alec?'

'Yes. All of a sudden.'

'You haven't had much of a chance, so far.'

'I wouldn't say that. Things have happened to jolt my ideas into proper perspective.'

'You faced the truth.'

'Maybe I did. But don't start drawing morals, Kate.'

'It has a moral for me.'

They were surrounded by darkness now, the lights in Willie's house pin-pointing behind them, the lights of the village still far ahead. On their left the river muttered sibilantly within its banks. On their right gloomed the ghostly mounds and bushes of the golf course.

Alec said: 'I'm not in your class, as far as morals are concerned. It's my biggest regret.'

'You're wrong.' She was glad of the darkness. 'You've been honest. I haven't.'

'You're probably the most honest person I've ever met.' He said it with conviction.

'I'm scared to tell you.'

'Then don't.'

'I must. You've got to know.'

'Why?'

'Oh, Alec, don't make it difficult! I want to be your—your friend, in the same way as Willie is, and I can't be that unless you know everything about me.'

Her hand touched his. He took it, tightening his fingers. 'Go on, then. I'm scared, too.'

'I knew it. All right. In my first year at the University I got married. I had a baby. It was still-born. My husband left me and I got a divorce. That's your do-gooding, golfing, schoolmarmish lady of the Manse. I gave up my married name. I've not been honest even about that.'

'You'd better let me have the details, Kate. You'll feel better afterwards. You taught me that piece of psychology, remember?'

'He was a boy I'd known in Egypt. His father was an English banker, his mother Egyptian. We were doing the same Arts course at Glasgow. He had plenty of money, which perhaps helps to explain why he was a bit of a philanderer, a bit of a drunkard. I thought I could steady him, perhaps cure him. I was wrong, of course.'

162

'You loved him?'

'I thought I did. I know now I didn't. I had a burning zeal to reform him. If I'd succeeded, I suppose my pride would have been insufferable.'

'Where is he now?'

'He went back to Egypt. He died three years ago. An alcoholic, leaving a widow. My parents were dead when it all happened, and I'm glad of that now. Harry knows, of course. He never blamed me.'

'Why should he? Neither do I.'

'Alec, when I was a girl I always dreamt of coming to my husband as a virgin. My gift to him. That did happen, of course. But now—well, if a man should say he loves me I have no gift for him.'

He stopped, and as he still held her hand she had to stop, too. They were past the Whinny Knowe, approaching the end of Riverside Street. The lights of the old houses were less than two hundred yards away.

'So that's what's worrying you.'

'You don't know what it means to a woman.'

'I can't answer that, Kate. Except to say that I—that I like you a lot better than I did. I thought you were rather the efficient, athletic type.' He laughed a little, to show he was exaggerating and making a joke. 'You're still inclined that way, of course. but now I know that behind it all you need encouragement and help just like—like ordinary folk, as Willie would say.'

'I do. Please help me, Alec.'

'I couldn't do no less, could I? After all you're done and are doing for me.'

She sighed. Her hand went slack in his.

He found it difficult to understand her mood. She was abasing herself for something she thought disgraceful but in which he could find nothing culpable. It seemed to him

163

that her standards must be so high that he could never hope to reach them. In this respect she was offering friendship on almost impossible terms.

She found it difficult to understand his mood. She wanted love and comfort. Yet his response to her appeal had been cool, with a hint than any help he might be willing to give her would be in repayment of a debt. Despite his talk of dreams, was he still in love with Jenny?

She took her hand from his and walked on. He followed.

She said: 'I hope our plan works.' It was 'our plan' now, he noticed. 'I wasn't being critical of the police when I worked it out. I'm just impatient to get all this ugliness over and done with, so that—so that you'll not be in danger any more.'

'I'm grateful, Kate. It might be a short-cut to the truth: I can see that. And the police certainly couldn't use the same amateur, "understand" methods. All the same . . .'

'We've been into all that.'

'I know. Sorry.'

They walked along Riverside Street in silence, turned into Fisher Row, entered the Main Street. People they met under the lights nodded, raised hats, touched caps, curious to see the minister's sister with Alec Fraser. Some smiled, as if with relief, and Alec discovered that to be with Kate was a passport out of suspicion. How many had heard, he wondered, about the attack on Jenny?

As they passed the Fraser Arms he glanced down at her, dark red head bobbing as she walked, making no attempt to keep step with him. Light from the front windows of the hotel fell on her face. He saw sadness there, and tenderness welled up in his heart. She tried so hard to be self-sufficient, independent, correct, to hide her loneliness and regret for a failure in love.

He searched for her hand, found it, held it.

She looked up, with a kind of happy surprise. 'People will see us.'

'Do you mind?'

'Not in the least.' She bent her head, as if inspecting the lifting toes of her flat and 'sensible' shoes. She laughed. 'But don't you realise that if two young people are seen walking hand-in-hand along Kilcolum Main Street they are immediately branded as loose-living and depraved?'

'The Semple influence.'

'Could be.'

Alec found himself grinning widely at a group of men gossiping on the pavement outside the public bar of the hotel. Two of them, he suddenly realised, had been in the same class with him at the village school. They grinned back, somewhat uneasily.

One of them said: 'Hullo, Alec.'

' 'Evening, Dave. Not a bad night.'

A mutter of talk in the group faded behind them. The street lamps petered out. They were climbing now on to the Manse road. Against a cloudy sky they could see the sycamores which sheltered the square and solid building.

Alec wanted to hold this mood for ever. It was as fresh and innocent as a newly opened flower. He had never expected to enjoy such a mood again. That it had come, unsought, lifted a lump to his throat.

Trees began to loom on either side, a thin wind rustling in their branches.

'Kate,' he said.

'Yes, Alec.' She was looking ahead, but seemed to move closer, her shoulder against his upper arm.

'D'you know the daft, extraordinary thing I've been thinking?'

She couldn't help smiling: he sounded so happy. 'I don't. Tell me.'

'I'd love to take you on at golf, give you a whale of a licking!'

'You couldn't! Not any more than Harry can.'

'I was once an extremely good golfer.'

'So Willie tells me. But so am I.'

'So Willie tells me!'

They laughed, as if it were all very funny, their clasped hands the junction through which flowed a current of pleasure. She was leaning against him now, their strides matching as he walked more slowly and she lengthened hers.

The current tingled in his body. He said: 'When all this is over, the day after tomorrow, I'll start practising, with Willie's expert assistance. Then you can expect the big challenge.'

'You haven't a hope, Alec. You're dreaming again.'

'I don't think so. This is the truth.'

They stopped, swung to each other. He saw her lips trembling, opening. Her body shaped itself to his. His heart was pounding, struggling against discipline.

A loose stone rattled. They heard steps approaching from the Manse. They stood apart. Alec was disappointed in a way, glad in another that his mood of anticipation should remain unbroken. There would be other times and other places.

'Harry!' said Kate.

Her brother came out of the dark, coatless, a college scarf with long ends hiding his dog-collar. 'Needed a breath of air. Thought I might meet you,' he said, concealing the fact that during the past half-hour he had become more and more worried by her absence.

'Alec brought me home,' she said, unnecessarily but

166

with a touch of pride. 'Willie was lazy.'

'Good. Won't you come in, Alec? Have a nightcap?'

'In a Manse?'

'Why not?'

'Come on.' She took his arm. 'Let's drink to that challenge.'

'I'd love to. Thanks a lot.'

They began to move towards the Manse gate.

'There's something I want to talk to you about,' said the Rev. Harry. 'I heard what happened to Jenny Craig: her father rang me. I went to see her. She seemed fine to me, but Dan Sillars was in a curious state. Moody. Angry. Like a caged animal.'

'He's had time to think.'

'I took him to his flat in my car, tried to calm him down. On the way he told me some astonishing things about Nancy MacKay!'

15

IT was a Thursday, but the village was so quiet it looked like a Sunday. The only busy, hurrying people were reporters and cameramen.

The funeral was to be at two o'clock, from the Allen house to the cluttered, moss-grown cemetery behind the church.

The school and all the shops were closed. The school would remain closed for the day, but at three in the afternoon, when the empty hearse returned and disappeared into Isaac Semple's yard, the shops would be open for business as usual. This was the day the new bread arrived from Glasgow. This was the day Kilcolum would be able to see itself and read about itself in avidly purchased newspapers.

When night came it would hear and see more on radio and television.

Inspector Greenlees held his morning conference at eleven. He looked serious and less bland than usual. Sergeant MacKinlay fiddled with papers, tapped a pencil-end on the table until his superior told him sharply to sit still.

'Tonight, then? You'll make an arrest tonight?' said the *Courier*, this morning without either Wellington boots or anorak because the sun was shining.

The inspector gave her a patient look. 'I told you, we're waiting for a final report from the lab in Stewarton. We hope to receive it late this afternoon. After that the Procurator Fiscal may decide we have enough evidence to justify an arrest.'

'What's the report about?'

'No comment.'

'Any hints, any clues as to the identity of the person you suspect?'

'None.'

It was a stone wall. The reporters and cameramen got up. Though feeling tense and frustrated—especially those working to a deadline for the evening papers—they made complimentary noises and indicated their gratitude, all of which they judged might encourage the inspector to talk to them more freely when the time came. They said 'Good morning' and went to snatch a drink and a meal before the funeral.

When they had gone, MacKinlay said: 'You're pretty sure now, sir?'

'Pretty sure. The report on the cloth fibres we found in

168

the girl's fingernails and on the bush beside the body ought to clinch it.'

'What first put you on the track, sir?'

MacKinlay was leaning back, genuinely interested. At the beginning he had tended to regard the inspector as an old square, commited to prehistoric methods of detection. Now he admitted to himself that Greenlees had taught him a thing or two—in general, that aside from technical advances the art of detection was the same as it had always been, an exercise in logic and character assessment.

'I'm not quite certain,' replied the inspector, by no means immune to this subtle kind of flattery, by no means averse to reading a lesson in police procedure to a young man he had once disliked but who now appeared to him a somewhat brash but distinctly promising member of the force. He made a mental note to include in his final report on the case a paragraph commending MacKinlay.

Smoothly he went on: 'I noticed at once, of course, that the atmosphere in Kilcolum was interesting, created, I judged, by conflict between old-fashioned social codes and modern attitudes. Then old Isaac Semple told us about the Cortina being in the village at the time of the murder, and this seemed to me a valuable pointer. So was the colour of the cloth fibres. Peter Fraser's evidence about the car was helpful, too, as was his admission this morning that Nancy MacKay had been his mistress.'

'There's something about Peter Fraser I never liked,' said MacKinlay. 'That poor little servant-girl, what he did to her ...'

'What did she do to him? It's a two-way traffic,' the inspector pointed out. 'However,' he continued, 'even before we knew about that youthful—er—liaison, I had become interested in Alec Fraser's story about finding the bracelet in his coat pocket. Did the person I suspected have an opportunity of putting it there? As you know, we discovered that he had.'

'Then my second interview with Grace Allen put us more in the picture?'

'Correct. And today, when I talked to Mrs Mac-Naughton, she added the final touches.'

'Sorry I missed the point the first time I spoke to Grace Allen.'

'My fault in a way. I should have told you how my mind was working.'

'Thank you, sir.' The sergeant did his best to preserve a serious mein. Quickly he added: 'Of course, the circumstances of the attack last night on Jenny Craig were also suggestive.'

'Certainly. And what she told you—her estimate of her assailant's height, strength, general characteristics—it all fitted in.' He paused, frowned. 'She had a narrow escape, that girl. Jenny Craig, I mean.'

'Quite, sir.'

The inspector heaved stout shoulders, discarding the burden of his thoughts. He said: 'So you see, MacKinlay, what you might call a hunch led to suspicion. Through the process of collating facts and discarding irrelevant detail, suspicion has now led to virtual certainty.'

'I'm glad it's nearly over. It's been an ugly business.'

'Obsession always is,' said Greenlees. He glanced at his watch. 'Half-past twelve. Time we had lunch. After the funeral you can take the car to Stewarton and try to hurry them up with that report.'

'Right, sir.'

'Fancy a beer before we go into the dining-room?'

'You bet.'

170

'It'll give us the opportunity of having another word with young Isaac. There's an aspect of his relationship with Nancy MacKay that still needs clearing up.'

The funeral came to an end with flowers frothing round a small grave and mourners weeping because of the sentiment in the minister's prayer. But discipline was maintained by old Isaac Semple, gaunt and towering in his undertaker's uniform of frock coat, striped trousers and black silk hat. The crowd dispersed. Tom and Grace Allen went back to a cold kitchen, though Mrs MacKay had left their table set for tea before going off to resume her work at the Big House.

Soon after six o'clock Sergeant MacKinlay returned from Stewarton with the lab report.

The inspector read through it, nodded. 'That's it, then. We'll have a meal. Then we might as well go and take him in.'

'As you say, sir.'

At half-past six, Kate, Willie and Alec met at the stone road bridge not far from the Big House. Darkness was almost complete, though light still lingered in the open sky to the west. They could hear the sea breaking gently in the distance.

Kate had on an unfashionable mackintosh, reaching almost to her ankles, with a dun-coloured scarf hiding her hair. 'I put the note in his letter-box myself, as soon as it got dark. Between seven and half-past, I said. On Columba's Crag.'

'I hope he doesna suspect anything,' said Willie, hoarsely. 'From the handwriting, say.'

'There was a grocery list Grace Allen had made out, that morning I was in her house. I remembered her way of

171

writing pretty well, I think. Anyway, I don't suppose he's had a note from her for years.'

'I'm not sure if I want to keep the appointment or not,' Alec said. 'You're determined to go through with this, Kate?'

'Of course.'

'Willie and I could go by ourselves ...'

'He might never show himself unless he saw a woman waiting, dressed like Grace Allen.'

Willie said: 'It's no good, Alec. She's as thrawn as they make them. Better get going, eh?'

'Well, whatever happens, Kate, we'll stick close to you.'

'I hope so, Alec.'

They left the road to the Big House and started to cross the fields, keeping to the shadowy hollows in case they were seen. Knowing every inch of the ground, Willie led the way, the others hard behind him. Kate was a good walker, sure-footed and quick even in the dark, but she clung to Alec's arm as if she were a fragile doll. He wasn't deceived. In any other circumstances he would have enjoyed himself.

Tonight the waxing moon rode among the stars in the eastern sky untrammelled by clouds. They had their backs to it as they approached Columba's Crag. In front, against the faint glimmer of the sea, the high cliff rose curved and rough, like a chipped scimitar blade.

There were small sounds, the scutter of a field-mouse, the distant sad mewing of a gull, the tiny scream of a vole perhaps in the death-grip of a weasel—all orchestrated against the regular mutter of the waves.

The night-scent came from dew-damp grass, muddy earth, peat-smoke thinned and freshened as it floated from the Big House.

172

Once they encountered a number of ewes, some lying down, some still cropping grass in a fold of ground sheltered by whins. The flock moved away at their approach, feet pattering, only small sounds of protest rattling in their throats as if they were unwilling to break the dark silence.

They squeezed through a fence and began to climb the Crag. Down on the rocks two oyster-catchers screamed and chattered in a bout of bad temper. Servants of St Bride they were called in the Gaelic. St. Bride must have been hard up for servants, thought Alec, having to make do with such unpleasant, argumentative birds.

There was a light from the east. It cooled them as they crouched on top of the Crag, recovering their breath.

Kate pulled back the right-hand cuff of her mackintosh and peered at the face of her wrist-watch. 'Ten to seven,' she said. 'Where are you two going to wait?'

About ten yards on the western side was a square boulder, behind it a hollow of turf scarred and fouled by sheltering sheep.

Willie pointed. 'Down there,' he said. 'It'll be in black shadow for the next hour, till the moon comes higher.'

'We'll have you in sight all the time,' Alec promised. 'Hear everything that's said. If anything happens we'll get to you in five seconds flat.'

'Keep well away from the edge,' advised Willie.

They moved down, carefully stooping, and took up position behind the boulder, kneeling there but able to see Kate as she got up and stood against the skyline. The air was motionless here, tainted with the smell of sheep droppings.

'Like the old days, Alec,' whispered Willie. 'Down by the burn.'

'Think he'll come?'

'If he reads the letter he will. He'll be desperate to keep Grace quiet.'

'He'll have murder in his mind.'

'I shouldna wonder. He killed once before. Maybe twice.'

'God, if Kate gets hurt . . .'

'How can she? We're here to make sure she isn't.'

'If this comes off, the case could be wrapped up to-night.'

'That's her whole idea. Finish it before any more harm's done. She's got spirit, that lassie.'

'Difficult girl to cope with.'

'In a way. Folk that are straight and direct are aye a bit troublesome.'

'I don't like her standing alone up there. In silhouette. What if he brings a gun?'

'Where would he get a gun? He never fired one in his life. He'll aim to use his hands, as he did before. Quick and quiet.'

'Poor Jenny! When I think . . .'

'Ssh! Listen.'

They froze against the boulder. Somewhere down on their right a sheep made a bubbling sound and ran off among the heather. Kate moved and looked in their direction.

'He's coming up this side.' Willie's voice, though scarcely audible, betrayed puzzled concern. 'He'll pass within a couple o' yards o' us.'

'I thought he'd take the way we did. It's an easier climb.'

'So did I. But he must have gone on, down past the Druid's Cave, keeping in the shadows.'

'Thinking he might surprise her?'

'Maybe.'

174

'He's delivered himself into our hands, Willie.'

A stone was dislodged some thirty feet down the slope. It rolled towards the edge of the cliff, spun over. Seconds later there was a faint thud as it struck the ground.

To anyone climbing, Alec and Willie were invisible, but Kate was a clear figure against the stars. It was obvious that she had heard the approaching sounds, but she stayed where she was, waiting.

A whin-bush, opposite the boulder and about ten yards away, seemed suddenly to spilt in two. But one of the parts was moving. Excited, Alec moved and cannoned into Willie. There was a small crunching sound as buttons on Willie's coat sleeve scraped against the base of the boulder. The dark shadow halted, merged with the ground. For a time there was uneasy quiet. A long wave broke and sighed on the rocks below. Alec held his breath.

Then the shadow was within two yards of them, crouched, its back to the moon, white blobs indicating clenched hands and an unrecognisable face among black clothes.

He saw them and turned and began to run, downhill.

'He musn't get away!' exclaimed Alec.

They leapt from behind the boulder, scrambling after him.

He was slow, a little too careful on the steep slope. Outdistancing Willie by a yard or so, Alec found himself on a narrow ridge of turf immediately above their quarry. He took a lungful of air and jumped and landed on top of the escaping man.

They rolled together, struggling, fingers searching at each other's throats. They struck a boulder, which jarred their bodies and left them gasping.

Willie slid down beside them, panting and cursing.

175

'Did you get him?'

'I've got him.'

Alec stood up, lugging his captive to his feet. Fighting for breath, a trickle of blood on his drawn white face, Dan Sillars stared back at them.

16

KATE heard the muffled sounds of pursuit and struggle receding down the slope. They grew faint, the thin wind carrying them away from her. Even an up-rush of voices was overwhelmed by the breaking waves.

The satisfaction in her sigh was tempered by mild disappointment. She was satisfied that her plan had been successful and that the murderer was now being dealt with by Alec and Willie. She was disappointed that she'd not been allowed to confront him first, to ask the vital questions which, in her view, so urgently required to be answered.

She moved towards the edge of the cliff, searching in the dark for an easy way down by which she could rejoin the others.

Behind her a harsh voice said: 'Grace!'

She halted, swung round, hands lifting to cover her breast. Blood thumped in her temples as she saw the black looming figure and recognised who it was.

'What's going on down there?' he demanded. Then he peered forward, took a step closer. 'You're not Grace!'

Her mind was dull, panic-stricken. She was alone with the murderer, her back to the airy margin of the cliff.

Alec and Willie were far away, fighting with someone else. One desperate thought intruded: *I must pretend to be calm, keep him talking until Alec comes.*

'So you got my letter?' she said.

He looked about him, like an animal in danger, making sure before he acted that his escape routes were clear. Sounds pulsed up from the sea. She could hear nothing on the western slope, where Alec was.

Forcing the words out, she said: 'You killed Mary Allen to get the bracelet, didn't you?'

His hands were rising, pale against the blur of his overcoat, fingers opening and closing.

'Your picture was in the locket part. You were afraid somebody might find out that Grace Allen was once your mistress.'

'She was a whore, like her cousin Nancy.' The voice came tight, controlled; the hands sagged stiffly down. 'I had no intention of killing her daughter, but when I stopped the girl on the street and asked for the bracelet she refused to give it up. I tried to take it. She struggled. I carried her off to the Whinny Knowe and killed her.' He took another step forward, his breath sickly on her face. 'How do *you* know all this?'

'Everybody knows it,' she lied, standing her ground, attempting to sound defiant though her knees were shaking. 'Twelve years ago, before Grace married, you were paying her well to sleep with you. But you were such a holy man, Isaac Semple, you would go to any lengths to keep it a secret. You were the Lord's elect. You could justify your behaviour to yourself, but for the sake of your reputation and your business you had to be careful.'

He was staring at her. She swallowed, dry-throated, and continued: 'The game must have gone on for some time, because one night, ten years ago, Alec Fraser and

177

Willie MacNaughton saw you down by the bridge. They suspected nothing, but they wondered why you didn't report them for poaching. The reason is plan. Grace was with you. Had you reported them the truth might have come out.'

He straightened up, took a long breath.

She was guessing now. She said: 'Then Nancy found out. She tried to blackmail you. She . . .'

'You don't know what she did!' His face was twisted, the sparse moonlight gouging out deep shadows on its surface. 'She—she seduced me, back yonder by the Ardcapple bridge, among the bushes and the grass. When it was over she laughed in my face and told me she now had a double hold on me. I would have to pay.'

Kate was weak with horror, the truth so sordid that she could scarcely take it in.

'She showed me the bracelet she'd got from some man. Nobody else knew about it, she said. I would have to give her an even more expensive one. Grace was loyal at least: I could trust her. But Nancy was evil, a scoffer, with no respect for age or dignity.'

He shuddered, then raised his voice. 'One night she came to me at the bridge and said she was with child—my child. I struck her with a stone and threw her into the river, breaking the rails to make it look as if she had fallen.' For a moment his snarl subsided. 'But not before I'd taken the bracelet,' he said.

A sob of disbelief shook Kate. 'You put your picture in the locket and gave it to Grace?'

'She was demanding more. I was getting tired of her. I gave her the bracelet and told her to keep it a secret between us. Tom Allen was beholden to me. He thought a lot of Grace. I arranged for them to marry.'

He lifted his head. Moonlight illumined his high

178

forehead, reminding Kate of a picture in a family Bible of Moses at prayer. But the holy look was suddenly distorted. 'What Nancy didn't tell me was that my grandson had been courting her, that she'd shown him the bracelet. When it didn't appear among her effects he—he suspected me. He didn't *know*, but he suspected. We had a quarrel. He reviled me. He accused me of being the father of her unborn child, of driving her to suicide. He didn't *know*, but I was an elder of the Church, a respectable business man. I—I had to give way to him.'

His eyes began to stray. He saw a stone lying loose on the turf. Kate saw it, too.

She said, abruptly: 'Did you know that Nancy hinted to her friend Mrs MacNaughton that Isaac Semple was responsible for the baby that was coming? Mrs Mac-Naughton thought she meant *young* Isaac . . .'

'But nobody stands in my way for long,' he whispered, almost to himself.

No longer interested in talk, he shambled suddenly to one side, picked up the stone, weighed it in his strong joiner's hand.

Hysteria threatened. 'You were at the Allens' that night.' she said, playing breathlessly for time. 'You saw Grace give Mary the bracelet. You stayed until it was time for her to be coming home from the Brownies. Then you stood in a doorway in the street, waylaid her.'

'That was what I did.' His eyes were glistening.

'Afterwards you tried to implicate Alec Fraser. After the service in the church you picked a row with him. With one hand you caught his shoulder. With the other you slipped the bracelet into his coat pocket. Last night you were down at the bridge and saw him with Jenny Craig. You took your chance . . .'

'He is worthless. A drug-addict, a fornicator. He is

179

damned!' The harsh voice skirled in hatred. Then it changed, mellowing into unction and a kind of reverence. 'But my soul is precious to the Lord,' he told her, 'because I came to Him in the days of my youth and innocence.'

She felt sick. 'You are a hypocrite, a living lie!' All caution was abandoned. 'Your holiness, it's an obscene sham . . .'

'No!'

He raised the stone and lunged at her. She screamed and stumbled to one side. Her foot caught in a tuft of grass. As she fell she saw him gaunt and lean above her, his overcoat flying open, his arm high.

She screamed again and thrust herself back. One foot found space. With cold fear she realised she was on the edge of the cliff.

'Alec!' she called. 'Oh, Alec!'

There was a pounding of footsteps. A shadow leapt on Isaac Semple. Hands wrenched back the upraised arm. The stone fell to the ground.

'I have him, sir!' exclaimed Sergeant MacKinlay, twisting the old man's arm with more force than perhaps was necessary.

As Greenlees emerged from the shadows, Alec, Willie and Dan Sillars came scrambling up on the other side. Alec ran to Kate, lifted her gently, held her close as she clutched at him and wept.

'Isaac Semple,' said the inspector, 'you are charged with the murder of Mary Allen. Anything you say may be used in evidence.'

Isaac was staring at Kate's quivering back. 'There's something she *didn't* know,' he said. 'I thought my picture was still in the bracelet. It wasn't. Grace must have destroyed it years ago.'

180

'But *we* knew that,' said MacKinlay. 'Lab tests showed that the locket part of the bracelet had been empty for a long time. Anyway, Grace Allen told me.'

'You old bastard!' exclaimed Dan Sillars, and he would have surged forward to strike him had not Willie kept hold of his arm. 'I knew it was you who attacked Jenny last night. She described you perfectly. I was on my way to your house tonight. I saw you coming and followed you. I'd have killed you myself . . .'

'Now, now, Mr Sillars,' interrupted Greenlees, 'that will be enough. Count yourself lucky that MacKinlay and I were also on our way to his house and followed you both here.'

Isaac Semple had begun to cry, groaning sobs racking his body.

'Take him away,' said the inspector.

'These religious maniacs,' muttered MacKinlay, snapping on the handcuffs, 'they're always the worst.'

On a sunny afternoon Commander Heathergill was checking accounts with Willie MacNaughton in the club-house. From the window they saw two people preparing to putt on the last green.

'Miss Kate and Alec Fraser,' said Willie. 'There's a big match on. Looks like it's still going.'

'Hrrmph. A fortnight in Kilcolum has done that young chap a power of good.'

They watched as Alec sank a longish putt and flung his putter in the air. Kate smiled, then turned to address her ball which lay less than two feet from the hole.

'She'll miss it,' said Willie.

'Nonsense!' snapped the Commander, eyebrows bristling. 'That's a tiddler for Kate Thomson.'

She missed it by several inches.

'What did I tell you, sir!'

'But look here...'

'She *let* him win,' explained Willie, as if dealing with a child. He sighed and shook his head in humble admiration. 'What a lassie!' he said.

'But—but in the name of golf . . .' The Commander broke off. 'Good God!' he spluttered.

The scene on the eighteenth green was enough to upset any Honorary Secretary. Flagstaff and clubs were scattered in confusion. Alec and Kate were kissing each other with obvious pleasure, heedless of curious eyes, heedless of damage to the precious, close-mown turf.

'Good God!' repeated the Commander. 'What goes on?'

'Human nature,' said Willie, with satisfaction.